TH

HAPPINESS

I think you may need a little air, Miss Dovedale," the Marquis murmured as he opened a window and guided Eugenia through.

The air made her stagger. She grasped hold of the ironwork that ran along the terrace and gazed misty eyed at the Marquis.

"It is all so – so – so wonderful," she breathed.

"I so am glad that you are – enjoying yourself," said the Marquis, his eyebrow raised.

"Oh, I am! Only – only one thing troubles me, my Lord."

The Marquis cocked his head enquiringly. At the same time his eyes travelled over her face and body with such undisguised hunger that she felt exultant. Why, she might yet have him!

She took a deep breath, and her mind seemed to swim in her head.

"You must not – you *really really* must not – marry Lady Walling."

A wry smile danced at the corners of the Marquis's lips. "Indeed? Then who *may* I marry, Miss Dovedale?"

Eugenia's eyes widened as if she imagined the Marquis a fool to ask.

"Why, me!" she beamed, brightly and innocently. "Me, Eugenia Dovedale."

And with that, she stumbled dazedly into his willing arms.

THE BARBARA CARTLAND PINK COLLECTION

Titles in this series

THE HOUSE OF HAPPINESS

BARBARA CARTLAND

Barbaracartland.com Ltd

THE BARBARA CARTLAND PINK COLLECTION

Barbara Cartland was the most prolific bestselling author in the history of the world. She was frequently in the Guinness Book of Records for writing more books in a year than any other living author. In fact her most amazing literary feat was when her publishers asked for more Barbara Cartland romances, she doubled her output from 10 books a year to over 20 books a year, when she was 77.

She went on writing continuously at this rate for 20 years and wrote her last book at the age of 97, thus completing 400 books between the ages of 77 and 97.

Her publishers finally could not keep up with this phenomenal output, so at her death she left 160 unpublished manuscripts, something again that no other author has ever achieved.

Now the exciting news is that these 160 original unpublished Barbara Cartland books are ready for publication and they will be published by Barbaracartland.com exclusively on the internet, as the web is the best possible way to reach so many Barbara Cartland readers around the world.

The 160 books will be published monthly and will be numbered in sequence.

The series is called the Pink Collection as a tribute to Barbara Cartland whose favourite colour was pink and it became very much her trademark over the years.

The Barbara Cartland Pink Collection is published only on the internet. Log on to www.barbaracartland.com to find out how you can purchase the books monthly as they are published, and take out a subscription that will ensure that all subsequent editions are delivered to you by mail order to your home.

If you do not have access to a computer you can write for information about the Pink Collection to the following address :

Barbara Cartland.com Ltd.
Camfield Place,
Hatfield,
Hertfordshire AL9 6JE
United Kingdom.

Telephone : +44 (0)1707 642629

Fax : +44 (0)1707 663041

THE LATE DAME BARBARA CARTLAND

Barbara Cartland who sadly died in May 2000 at the age of nearly 99 was the world's most famous romantic novelist who wrote 723 books in her lifetime with worldwide sales of over 1 billion copies and her books were translated into 36 different languages.

As well as romantic novels, she wrote historical biographies, 6 autobiographies, theatrical plays, books of advice on life, love, vitamins and cookery. She also found time to be a political speaker and television and radio personality.

She wrote her first book at the age of 21 and this was called *Jigsaw*. It became an immediate bestseller and sold 100,000 copies in hardback and was translated into 6 different languages. She wrote continuously throughout her life, writing bestsellers for an astonishing 76 years. Her books have always been immensely popular in the United States, where in 1976 her current books were at numbers 1 & 2 in the B. Dalton bestsellers list, a feat never achieved before or since by any author.

Barbara Cartland became a legend in her own lifetime and will be best remembered for her wonderful romantic novels, so loved by her millions of readers throughout the world.

Her books will always be treasured for their moral message, her pure and innocent heroines, her good looking and dashing heroes and above all her belief that the power of love is more important than anything else in everyone's life.

"Love has inspired great poets, artists and architects throughout the ages. Love can inspire anyone to greater heights than could ever be possibly imagined"

Barbara Cartland

CHAPTER ONE
1835

Eugenia Dovedale mounted the stairs carefully, feeling for each step with her dainty foot. She was bringing tea to her great-aunt and she was terrified of dropping the large, mahogany tray.

Great-Aunt Cloris took a nap every afternoon. At four o'clock precisely she liked to be awakened by Eugenia. There was a maid, Bridget, who prepared the tray, placing on it the silver pot and jug and sugar bowl, but it was Eugenia who was expected to carry the tray all the way up from the basement to the second floor, where Great-Aunt Cloris slumbered in her large, rosewood bed.

Eugenia reached her great-aunt's room. She pushed open the door with her elbow and stepped inside.

"Is that you, Eugeeenia?"

She had wanted her great-niece named after her. When this desire was not gratified, the old lady had for ever after affected to be unable to pronounce the 'french-sounding' Eugenia.

"Yes, Great-Aunt Cloris, it is me."

"Did you bring me the shortbread from Fortnum's?"

"Yes, great-aunt."

"Excellent. Would you pour my tea, please?"

Eugenia picked up the silver pot and poured.

"Yes. Is that all?"

Great-Aunt Cloris peered at her great-niece. "You are anxious to escape me?"

"Oh, no. It's just that Mama requested that I join *her* for tea today."

She looked disgruntled. "Oh, well, of course, you must take tea with your Mama."

Eugenia turned to go.

"Eugeeeenia?"

"Yes, Great-Aunt?"

"You may take one piece of shortbread. To share with your Mama."

Eugenia descended the stairs with the shortbread wrapped in a napkin.

Mrs. Dovedale was sitting before the fire in the little first floor parlour that she and Eugenia shared. She looked up as her daughter entered.

"What have you got there, Eugenia?"

"Shortbread. From Great-Aunt Cloris."

"Just one piece between the two of us?"

"I don't really want any, Mama."

"I suppose it's from Fortnum's?"

"Yes, Mama. I bought it there yesterday."

Mrs. Dovedale heaved a dramatic sigh. "That I should live to see my daughter treated as a servant!"

"But I am not, Mama. I *enjoy* going to Fortnum's."

"That is beside the point. You are run off your feet doing errands for that old lady."

"But Mama, I am grateful to her. She gave us a home."

"A home? You call this a home? When we are given a quota of coal a day, like scullery maids? When our meals are rationed and our sherry watered? When you cannot go out into Society because the old skinflint won't open her purse to buy you so much as a pair of gloves?"

Eugenia said nothing. She picked up the poker and prodded the fire. A meagre flame spluttered in the grate.

"If it was not for my good friend, Lady Granton, you would hardly know what Society was!" lamented Mrs. Dovedale. "You would not know how to address an Earl, or wield a fan, or hold a fork in the correct manner."

Eugenia suppressed a smile. Mrs. Dovedale seemed to forget that it was she herself, so full of ambition for her daughter, who had long ago taught Eugenia the appropriate social skills.

Great-Aunt Cloris was well-meaning, but hers was a notoriously frugal and austere household. Lady Granton often invited Eugenia and her mother to tea and it was at these sessions that Eugenia now and then met people of her own age.

"To think I once wore satin and took tea with a Marquis!" Mrs. Dovedale continued. "To think I was once Mistress of my own house, with my own maid and a set of copper pans!"

Eugenia shifted in her chair. She knew what was coming next. A descant on the privileged life that the Dovedale family once lived in Rutland, where Mr. Dovedale was Head Steward on the Marquis of Buckbury's estate, Buckbury Abbey.

Buckbury was one of the grandest houses in Rutland. The first Marquis had been a General, a favourite of King Henry VIII and had been granted the vast lands in the North at the Dissolution of the Monasteries.

The present Marquis was as handsome as his father. It was a great shame that he no longer lived in England, but on his late mother's estate near the Alps. Though why he should prefer a no doubt draughty chateau in the wilds of France to the delights of Buckbury was beyond Mrs. Dovedale.

"Such a life he led at Buckbury," trilled Mrs.

Dovedale. "The garden parties in the summer – the boats on the lake at dusk, their lanterns gleaming – the huge log fires in all the rooms in winter – the carriages rolling along the drive for the balls – the chandeliers sparkling. The Christmas parties to which the staff were always invited. Your father and I were accorded pride of place at the supper table. The Marquis was such a generous host. And the last party he held there, you were invited too. Do you remember?"

Eugenia was wriggling her toes before the fire. Her slippers were worn and did not keep out the cold.

"I remember, Mama."

How could she forget? Even if her mother was not continually reminding her, the image of Buckbury Abbey that Christmas was engraved on her mind.

Ten years old, she had stood awe-struck at the sight of the tree in the hall. It seemed to go on forever – as high as the minstrel's gallery. Candles flickered on every branch and the red baubles glowed in their light. Far, far away – right at the top – a silver star gleamed.

Eugenia had crept up to the minstrel's gallery and leaned over the balustrade. The top of the tree was now on a level with her eyes. Standing on her tiptoes, she stretched out her hand, trying to reach the Christmas star.

"What are you doing, young lady?" a voice had gently asked.

Eugenia did not recognise the Marquis for a moment.

This tall gentleman in a gleaming, braided jacket and elegant white gloves took her breath away.

"I – wanted to touch the star," she explained. "To see if it was icy. Because then I would know it was a *real* star."

The Marquis looked amused. "Well, I am afraid to tell you that it is not a real star. Real stars are very hard to come by. You have to be lucky and find one where it falls. No,

4

that is a star made of silver. And I should hate to see you fall trying to touch it."

Eugenia detected the mild tone of reproof. "Oh, I shan't trouble to try now I know," she assured the Marquis.

"I am glad to hear it."

Eugenia regarded the Marquis with her head on one side. "You look like a Prince in that costume," she said.

"And you, mademoiselle, look like a Princess," laughed the Marquis.

It was true, Eugenia did look enchanting. Her hair fell to her waist like a red-gold mantle and her eyes resembled large, blue water lilies. She was dressed in blue muslin and on her feet she wore a pair of blue satin slippers.

"Thank you. This dress looks very nice if I twirl. Shall I twirl for you?"

"Please do," answered the Marquis.

"Eugenia, what are you doing?" Mrs. Dovedale, puffing up the gallery stairs, had stopped in astonishment at the sight of her daughter's pirouette.

"Nothing, Mama."

"You were twirling. That is not very lady-like. Please apologise to the Marquis."

"But I did ask him first," protested Eugenia.

"I can assure you, Mrs. Dovedale, she did," confirmed the Marquis, a twinkle in his eye.

Mrs. Dovedale took Eugenia's hand and began to lead her away. But Eugenia tugged her hand free and ran back to the Marquis.

"Mr. Marquis," she said, "one day I will marry you and no one else in the world!"

"Eugenia!" exclaimed Mrs. Dovedale.

The Marquis, meanwhile, regarded the little girl before him with a sober air.

"In that case," he replied, "I shall be sure to wait for you to grow up."

The snap of a log in the fire brought Eugenia back from her reverie.

Uncomplaining as she was, she could not but be aware of the difference between the remembered scene at warm, glowing Buckbury and this little parlour in London, with its shabby armchairs and patched curtains at the windows.

Mrs. Dovedale, as if she had been privy to her daughter's thoughts, was chiming out the very words that had just rung in Eugenia's head.

"*In that case, I shall be sure to wait for you to grow up*". That is what the Marquis said. He didn't, of course. Wait, I mean. What can one expect?" Mrs. Dovedale sniffed. "That Countess was determined to have him."

The Countess had been very beautiful. A younger friend of the Marquis's late mother, she had arrived at Buckbury a month after the Christmas Ball.

When she returned to France a fortnight later, the Marquis had followed.

He had informed his Head Steward that there were family problems to deal with in France and he would be away for some time. Mrs. Dovedale, however, was convinced that the Marquis was in hot pursuit of the Countess.

Whatever the true reasons for the Marquis's departure, Buckbury Abbey was to all intents and purposes closed. There were no more garden parties, no more balls.

"What a paradise we lost!" mourned Mrs. Dovedale. "What a world we are reduced to now!"

Listening to her mother, Eugenia could not help but marvel that her mother appeared to have forgotten her own part in the dissolution of her former life.

The truth was, with Buckbury shut and life a good deal duller, Mrs. Dovedale had begun to chafe at her lot.

As the months dragged by and there was no sign of the Marquis, she became fractious. She began to chivvy her long-suffering husband. Had he no ambition other than Head Steward of a silent house and ghostly estate? Finally she convinced him that he was destined for greater things. All he needed was money to establish himself in some business enterprise or other.

He resigned his Head Stewardship and sailed for the gold-panning fields of Alaska.

His wife and daughter were sent to lodge with his widowed Aunt Cloris in London.

In less than six months, word reached them that Mr. Dovedale was dead of a fever. Mrs. Dovedale and Eugenia never returned to Buckbury Abbey.

"Never to return home," Mrs. Dovedale was still rambling, moved to tears now by her own reminiscing, "never to see our '*Paragon*' again – so aptly named, such a haven was it from the rush of the world."

Eugenia, elbow on the arm of her chair, leaned her chin in her hand and stared into the fire.

It was '*Paragon*' that she missed most whenever she thought of her past.

Nestling deep in the woods at Buckbury, '*Paragon*' was the lovely rambling cottage where the Head Steward and his family lived. Climbing roses covered its walls, doves circled its eaves. Deer nibbled at the long grass beyond its white fence.

Eugenia had owned a cat called Sugar and a little pony called Bud.

She had been so happy at '*Paragon*' with her dear Papa, so happy that she tried not to think about it.

If only her mother would not so constantly remind her!

For Mrs. Dovedale, the only route out of her straightened circumstances was Eugenia. The girl was so beautiful, everybody said so. She could ensnare the Prince of Wales himself if she wished!

Mrs. Dovedale plotted and planned for Eugenia to be noticed. Not a man with half a name for himself passed within the mother's orbit, but he was extolling the virtues of her daughter. Not one name of an eligible bachelor could drop from Lady Granton's lips but that Mrs. Dovedale was trying to effect an introduction.

Mrs. Dovedale would accompany Eugenia on errands to Fortnum's for the sole purpose of pointing out Lord this or Earl that to her daughter. During walks in Kensington Gardens she would nudge Eugenia's elbow at every haughty Viscount or Duke who rode by.

"Throw him a glance, my dear. Turn your profile to him. Step into his path."

Her mother's machinations made Eugenia miserable. She began to form an instinctive resistance to any romantic suggestion that her mother made.

Leaning her forehead on the windowpane, Eugenia murmured to herself the familiar words that worked upon her resolve like a daily mantra.

"*I will never, never marry anyone of whom my mother approves!*"

*

Seated at breakfast, reading the newspaper through her lorgnette, Mrs. Dovedale gave a sudden squawk of excitement.

"Mama?"

Mrs. Dovedale waved her hand before her face, as if whatever she had read had brought on a sudden heat. "Oh, my goodness, oh, my goodness, we are saved!"

Eugenia stared. "How exactly are we saved, Mama?"

She threw down the paper and pointed. "There. There. Do you see? The Marquis of Buckbury has returned to England and is *at this very moment in London*!"

Eugenia, guessing the cast of her mother's mind, frowned. "He must be very *old* and *grey* by now."

"Old? Grey? He can't be more than – let me see – he was twenty one when last I saw him – you were ten – why, he's barely more than thirty now!"

"Ancient," sighed Eugenia.

Mrs. Dovdedale was not listening.

"I must make sure that he is invited to one of Lady Granton's soirées," she continued. "She would surely do it for us. He is bound to come if he hears that the widow of his old Head Steward is present. He cannot have forgotten us. He cannot have forgotten *you*!"

"Of course he has forgotten me. And even if he hasn't, what is all this to do with us being saved?"

Mrs. Dovedale looked coy. "Why, you were so taken with each other at that Christmas party – "

"Mama, I was *ten*!"

"But it was obvious that you were going to blossom into a real beauty." her mother persisted. "He said he would wait – "

Eugenia raised an eyebrow. "Mama, I think you are forgetting the Countess!"

"Oh, yes, the Countess." Mrs. Dovedale sank into her chair for a moment before brightening. "Even so, once reacquainted, the Marquis is bound to want to do something for you."

"Not charity!" replied Eugenia sharply.

Mrs. Dovedale threw up her hands and rose from the table. "Eugenia, I despair of you, I really do! I have no idea what it is you really want." With that, she sailed from the room.

What did she really want? Passion! She did not want whatever beauty she might possess bartered for a string of pearls and a horse and carriage. She did not want a pompous Earl or a dreary old Marquis. She wanted to be swept off her feet by someone for whom romance was more important than position, for whom the call of the heart was stronger than the call of duty.

Her eyes closed for a moment as she imagined this wild and impetuous lover.

He was most definitely *not* someone of whom her mother would approve!

She hoped that her obvious lack of enthusiasm had discouraged her mother from plotting an encounter with the Marquis of Buckbury.

Mrs. Dovedale, however, was not a woman to be dissuaded from any course of action she had decided upon.

Two days later she entered Eugenia's room in triumph.

"We are to attend Lady Granton's on Tuesday. The Marquis of Buckbury will be present. This will be your first evening soirée."

Eugenia did not look up from her book. "I cannot go. I have nothing to wear."

"Oh, you are not to worry about that," Mrs. Dovedale shot back. "I shall take in my old ball-gown."

Eugenia turned the page. "Then I shall look like a fool."

"Look like a fool? Of course you won't look like a fool."

Mrs. Dovedale, however, was proved quite wrong. On the day of the soirée, even Great-Aunt Cloris, so approving of hand-me-downs, pursed her lips.

"What is this colour, Florence?" she asked.

"Pigeon breast blue," she replied.

"Pigeon breast blue?" Great-Aunt Cloris looked doubtful. "Then it has greatly faded."

"Faded? Nonsense. It resembles the underside of a flower."

"More like the underside of a stale loaf!"

Eugenia, standing before her great-aunt's pier glass, took a grim satisfaction in this exchange.

The dress was indeed the colour of a stale loaf, grey and unflattering. Not only that, it was almost perversely out of fashion.

She suppressed a sudden giggle. What did she care? She had no wish to impress the Marquis of Buckbury or anyone else at Lady Granton's soirée.

She knew her appearance would invite ridicule and convinced herself that she would not mind. Anything rather than serve her mother's purpose.

Mrs. Dovedale, who would have thought her daughter was perfection in a workhouse shift or a cook's apron, was meanwhile unperturbed by Great-Aunt Cloris's remarks.

"All it needs is a touch of something – " she regarded Great-Aunt Cloris slyly. "A pretty shawl, now, would do the trick."

Great-Aunt Cloris struggled.

"She may borrow my Chinese silk," she said at last, grudgingly.

Eugenia shook her head. "Oh, great-aunt, I really don't – "

"Now don't be ungrateful, child," she said quickly. "Take it, before I change my mind."

The shawl was a master stroke by Mrs. Dovedale. Its rosy hue softened the harsh effect of the dress. The cobalt flowers with which it was embroidered matched the dark blue iris of Eugenia's eyes.

For her mother, Eugenia's natural charms shone undimmed.

Nevertheless, when she and Eugenia entered Lady Granton's drawing room in Cavendish Square, the sharp intake of collective breath was not immediately one of admiration.

"Come on, Eugenia," said Mrs. Dovedale, "don't hang back."

Eugenia advanced into the room, head high. Her grace was unmistakable. So too, in the amber light from the lamps, was the soft lustre of her skin. Her hair was a crown of gold and her eyes glimmered like sapphires. The dowdy, old-fashioned dress served only to heighten her timeless beauty.

The gentlemen present surged forward, agog, to introduce themselves to the new arrival.

At the far end of the room, double doors led into Lord Granton's library. Lord and Lady Granton now emerged through these doors. With them walked a tall gentlemen of unmistakably aristocratic mien. His forehead was high, his grey eyes keen and intelligent. His dark brows almost met over a fine, chiselled nose. If there was one fault about his features, it was that they suggested a certain severity of character. Otherwise he was the epitome of a handsome, distinguished gentleman of the world.

His gaze roved over the assembled company of young ladies. Not one of them pleased his eye. The ladies, however, once aware of his presence, fluttered their lashes and fans wildly in his direction.

Eugenia was invisible amidst her own throng of admirers.

"There appears to be an incident of sorts over by the door," remarked Lord Granton. He chuckled. "Daresay

Miss Dovedale is in the middle of that scrum."

The tall gentleman raised an eyebrow. "Dovedale?"

"A spirited young lass," added Lord Granton.

The gentleman turned his head towards the door. "Dovedale?" he repeated.

Lady Granton seized on his interest. "Would you care to be introduced?"

The gentleman inclined his head. "Very much," he replied.

The young men around Eugenia fell away as Lady Granton and the Marquis approached.

"Lady Granton – how d'you do – most kind – excellent sherry, Lady Granton – " they choroused.

Hearing Lady Granton's name, Mrs. Dovedale turned from rearranging the shawl about Eugenia's shoulders. When she saw the distinguished gentleman who accompanied her friend, she gave a screech.

"The Marquis! It is the Marquis."

Eugenia, half hidden behind her mother, froze.

"The Marquis!" cried Mrs. Dovedale again. "Oh, what a very great pleasure it is to see you again."

The Marquis of Buckbury – for this was indeed the identity of the gentleman – bent his head graciously.

"Mrs. Dovedale, I suspected it might be you."

"Oh, it is I, indeed it is I," preened Mrs. Dovedale as she dropped a belated curtsy. "And much changed you will find me, I am sure. I have been blown all about by the storms of fortune and pinioned most unhappily on the rocks of circumstance."

"Indeed," intoned the Marquis gravely.

"There remains one treasure, however, that the cruel hand of fate has not snatched from me," continued her mother. "One treasure that brightens my day and gives me hope for the future. My daughter here. Eugenia."

She stepped aside and motioned towards Eugenia. The Marquis looked politely on. Eugenia's head was bent so low that all he could see of her was a coil of golden hair.

Mrs. Dovedale gave a little laugh. "The dear creature is so shy! *Eugenia*!"

Without looking up, Eugenia sank in an obedient but exaggerated curtsy to the floor. There she remained, her skirts rising about her like a grey flood.

"Miss Dovedale," said the Marquis, extending his hand.

Eugenia placed her hand reluctantly in that of the Marquis. As he drew her to her feet she was forced at last to meet his gaze.

The Marquis started as if struck.

"A treasure indeed," he murmured.

Lady Granton and Mrs. Dovedale nodded in satisfaction.

Still the Marquis stared. Eugenia felt her cheeks begin to burn under his intense scrutiny.

"She is my pride and joy," gushed Mrs. Dovedale. "No one could have a better daughter. So considerate, so loving, so devoted."

"And spirited, I hear," said the Marquis softly, his eyes still on Eugenia.

Mrs. Dovedale looked instantly alarmed. "Spirited? Nonsense! Where did you hear that? She is as tame as a canary. She wouldn't say boo to a goose."

Eugenia's eyes flashed for a second. "Mama! Please!"

"What, daughter? What have I said? Only the truth! The Marquis knows how to take me. I always spoke the truth." Mrs. Dovedale looked craftily at the Marquis. "I daresay your own wife is a woman of no spirit, too, and the Lord be thanked for it."

The Marquis frowned. "My own wife – ?"

"You married, did you not? I seem to remember a Countess?"

A shadow crossed the Marquis's brow. "No," he said shortly. "I married no one."

Mrs. Dovedale trembled with the effort of concealing her excitement. "A bachelor. Well, well, well."

Lady Granton, aware at last of Eugenia's growing discomfort, felt it necessary to intervene.

"I am sure, my Lord, you are ready for some refreshment," she said. "There is a buffet laid out in the dining room."

"Eugenia should partake as well," cried Mrs. Dovedale. "She eats like a bird."

The Marquis held out his arm to Eugenia.

"Permit me," he offered.

Eugenia hesitated but, at a discreet prod from her mother, took the Marquis's arm.

Eugenia was determined to maintain an air of disinterest but, on entering the dining room, her eyes widened at the sight of the groaning table. There were small tartlets of chicken and mushroom and anchovy. Whole hams and suckling pigs with apples in their mouths. Pyramids of glacé fruits and silver bowls of syllabub.

She had never seen such a delightful display.

Mrs. Dovedale, moving up behind them, exclaimed in delight.

The Marquis, meanwhile, observed Eugenia with interest. "You often attend these soirées given by Lady Granton?"

"No. I – we – just come to tea. We sit around the silver urn and eat muffins."

Eugenia began to fill her plate. Eager to taste all the delicacies that were usually denied her, her hand flew hither and thither over the table.

The Marquis watched with amusement.

Mrs. Dovedale grew uneasy. "Ah – something has stirred her appetite tonight. Most curious."

Soon the titbits on Eugenia's plate threatened to topple.

"Eugenia, dear, I do think that is enough," urged her mother anxiously. "I am sure you do not wish the Marquis to think you are – that you have suddenly developed – inordinate tastes – "

"But Mama – there are so many delicious things here!"

Eugenia took a hearty bite of anchovy tart.

Horrified, Mrs. Dovedale plucked at the Marquis's arm, anxious to distract him from what she considered to be a most indecorous sight.

"I am sure we are – ahem – all happy to welcome the Marquis back to England," she said.

The Marquis bowed. "I am happy to return, now that my duties in Europe are at an end."

"Duties?" repeated Mrs. Dovedale blankly.

"My cousin and his wife in France were killed and I was made guardian of their children. I intended to bring them back to live at Buckbury, but it was soon apparent that to wrench them from the home they knew and loved would be cruel. So I remained in France to oversee their education. Now they are young adults and – it is time for me to come home."

"By that you mean Buckbury?" Mrs. Dovedale probed.

"I do. Of course, I have the London house, in Lansdowne Square. But it is Buckbury that is my real home."

Mrs. Dovedale clasped her hands together. "Ah, and what an Eden Buckbury Abbey was for us. You have no idea."

The Marquis frowned. "I knew that Mr. Dovedale enjoyed the life there. That is why I was so surprised that he chose to leave."

Mrs. Dovedale coughed. "It was different – after you departed. And my husband felt he needed – to rise in the world."

"I see." The Marquis's eyes strayed back to Eugenia.

Mrs. Dovedale nearly fainted as she saw Eugenia about to place a very large glacé fruit in her mouth.

"You are neglecting the Marquis, who was so kind as to escort you in to supper," chided Mrs. Dovedale.

"I am sorry, Mama."

Mrs. Dovedale turned back to the Marquis.

"As I was saying, Marquis, Buckbury Abbey was like a paradise to us. I remember all the wonderful parties that you gave. We so enjoyed watching the fine ladies and gentlemen arrive in their carriages. And oh, how the house was lit up at Christmas! You remember that, don't you, Eugenia?"

"Yes, Mama."

"The last Christmas that you were in residence, Marquis, was the first party that Eugenia attended."

"I remember," said the Marquis. The look that he now cast on Eugenia was unmistakably tender. "I came upon her in the minstrel's gallery. She was attempting to touch the star at the top of the Christmas tree."

Mrs. Dovedale clapped her hands, delighted at the turn

17

in the conversation. "That would be Eugenia. Such a droll creature she was!"

Eugenia felt her cheeks begin to flush again.

"And do you remember, Marquis, what she said to you?"

Eugenia's flush deepened. *'Please, Mama, no!'* she prayed silently but her prayers went unheeded.

"*'Mr. Marquis, I will marry you and no one else in the whole world!'*"cried Mrs Dovedale. "That is what she said. And you replied *'in that case, I shall be sure to wait until you are grown-up'*."

"I remember," rejoined the Marquis gravely.

Eugenia's lips trembled as she spoke,

"But all that, sir, was when I was much, much younger. As," she added in a lower voice, "were you."

There was a shocked silence before the Marquis gave a curt bow.

"Madam – Miss Dovedale," was all he said, before turning and making his way out of the dining room.

For a moment, Eugenia felt a fleeting sense of shame.

This was quickly dispelled as Mrs. Dovedale gave a low moan and staggered to a chair.

"What have you done, Eugenia? It was all going so well. You have destroyed all my hopes. A bachelor! So wealthy! And he was interested in you. Oh, what have you done? Why do you always sabotage me?"

As her mother swayed and clutched her bosom in despair, Eugenia's shame fled. All she felt, staring at her mother, was a sense of grim triumph.

Once again she had managed to thwart yet another of her odious plans!

CHAPTER TWO

For days after the soirée, Mrs. Dovedale kept to her bed. She rang her bell frequently for attention but Eugenia knew better than to answer. Instead she would open the parlour door and watch Bridget toil up the stairs with warming pans, broth, toast and hot water with lemon. Bridget would shoot accusatory looks at Eugenia. All this extra work, just because Miss could not bring herself to be civil to a Marquis. A Marquis, mind you!

Her father had always said, "whatever you do in life, follow your heart and you cannot go wrong." Her mother wanted her to behave as if she had no heart!

She had taken Great-Aunt Cloris her tea at three o'clock. There remained nothing more for her to do until supper, when her great-aunt would deign to descend to join Eugenia for mutton stew or cold ham.

Eugenia had been surprised at Great-Aunt Cloris's reaction to the story of herself and the Marquis, as related by her mother.

"The child has sense, Florence. Her father was a High Steward and her mother's family were in trade. Marquises are quite out of her league."

Mrs. Dovedale had fled wailing from the room –

Eugenia gave a little smile at the memory and pressed her forehead to the window.

Two young ladies were out for a stroll, their cloaks thrown over their shoulders. Eugenia could hear the clack of their heels on the pavement.

She watched them longingly. No doubt they were on their way to Kensington Gardens. She and her mother were wont to take a walk there every day after lunch, but since Mrs. Dovedale had been confined to bed, this pleasure had been denied her daughter.

Eugenia frowned.

She was sent on errands by her great-aunt without her mother (although to be sure Bridget or the scullery maid would always be trailing behind her with the basket). She could not see why she should not go to Kensington Gardens alone.

The thought was father to the deed. Without further ado, Eugenia tiptoed down the stairs and retrieved her coat from its hook in the cloakroom. She pinned on her hat before the hall mirror. Then she quietly opened the front door and slipped out.

She felt like a bird let loose from its cage as she sped along the street.

The Bayswater Road was busy. She held on to her hat as she crossed, dodging the carts and carriages. A newsboy whistled at her over his bundle of papers.

The gardens seemed peaceful after the fray of the streets. There were not many people about but Eugenia was too exhilarated to be wary. She was alone and free!

She turned her head at the sound of hooves. Two figures on horseback rode amidst the trees to her right. Beyond them, to the South, lights were beginning to twinkle on Kensington Gore.

It was nearly dusk. Eugenia had never been out alone this late.

A voice from the shadowy verge startled her.

"Going somewhere nice, lady?"

A man stepped out into her path, forcing her to halt. His manner of addressing her had indicated that he was no gentleman and this was confirmed by his demeanour. His eyes gleamed with insolence. She shuddered as he bared a row of stained and broken teeth.

"Going somewhere nice?" he repeated.

Eugenia made to pass but he put a hand on her arm to detain her.

"Why such a hurry? There's nothing that way but the Serpentine. Are you by any chance meeting someone there for a *rendee-voo*?"

"N-no," replied Eugenia. "I was just – I am just – walking."

She shrugged off his hand and moved on. To her horror, the man fell into step beside her.

"I have no need of company," Eugenia remarked coldly.

"Oh, but you do," leered the man. "All on your own in the park at dusk. Tsk, tsk. Lucky you've knocked into a gentleman of leisure. I can go wherever my fancy takes me. And this evening it takes me in your direction, so it does."

Eugenia quickened her step, throwing anxious glances about her. The light was fading fast and the park was nearly empty. Ahead of her on the bridge she could make out two horses, standing motionless under a gas lamp. Their riders had alighted. One, obviously a manservant, stood holding the bridles. The other leaned on the balustrade, smoking and gazing down at the darkening surface of the Serpentine. Otherwise Eugenia was alone with her unwelcome companion.

"Slow down a little, won't you?" he huffed.

"I must go home," cried Eugenia, desperately "I must go home."

The man caught her arm and she stumbled to a halt.

"Come on, no more of this racing. Take off the old chapeau and lets have a good look at you."

Eugenia gave a cry as he tugged at her hat. Loosened pins fell to the grass and strands of hair uncoiled.

The man whistled. "I've hooked a right beauty and no mistake," he said.

"Give me back my h-hat, please!"

"Tell you what, I'll give it back if you give me a kiss."

"No," said Eugenia in alarm. "Certainly not."

The man lunged at her greedily, pinning her arms to her side. "Go on, don't be a tease."

"No!" Eugenia struggled as she felt cold lips seek her mouth. "NO!"

"Unhand the young lady at once!"

The voice that rang from the bridge ahead was one of such natural command that the man released Eugenia immediately.

The owner of the voice tossed aside his cigar and strode angrily towards them. Eugenia's companion began to back away.

"Just – a little fun, guvnor!" he bleated.

With that he turned on his heels and fled.

Dazed, Eugenia knelt to retrieve her hat.

"Madam, are you all right?"

A firm hand under her elbow helped her to her feet.

"I – yes – thank you. I am. Thank you."

Setting her hat on her head, Eugenia raised grateful eyes to her rescuer. When she saw who it was, she gave a cry.

The Marquis of Buckbury!

The Marquis started in his turn. "Miss Dovedale – "

Hands suddenly shaking, Eugenia felt for her veil. "Yes. It's me. Only I wish it wasn't. Oh, how I wish it wasn't."

"Miss Dovedale, I – "

"No. Please. Don't say a word. And if you ever see Mama – please – don't say a word. She would be so cross. But you see, she would not leave her bed – oh, where *is* my veil? – and I so much wanted to walk – and it was wonderful. I felt so free, and the air was so cool – it was wonderful until that man – that horrible man – I didn't know him – really I didn't – I didn't know him at all – "

The Marquis had gazed on in silence while Eugenia, eyes brimming with unshed tears, struggled to explain herself and untangle her veil at the same time.

"Permit me," he now offered gently.

Eugenia stood trembling as the Marquis unwound her veil from the crown of her hat. She was too embarrassed to look at him.

"There." The Marquis stepped back and bowed. "It is done."

"T-thank you." Cheeks aflame, Eugenia quickly drew down the veil.

"You will, of course, allow me to escort you home," offered the Marquis, signalling to his manservant on the bridge.

Eugenia recoiled in alarm. "I c-can't. If Mama should see me! I can't."

With that, she picked up her skirts and turned to run.

"Miss Dovedale!" The Marquis's voice rang out behind her but she only ran the faster.

The Marquis stared after her. Then, spinning on his heels, he strode swiftly to the bridge where his horse and manservant waited.

Eugenia, in her flight, stumbled once or twice but otherwise never paused. Breast heaving, hair streaming from under her hat, she at last saw the lights of the Bayswater Road ahead.

She never once looked back at the park, never once observed the two riders who followed at a distance, determined to see that Miss Eugenia Dovedale reached home in safety. Not till Eugenia paused before her great-aunt's house in Craven Hill did this discreet escort turn away.

The lamps were lit in the rooms of both her mother and her great-aunt. That meant that they were awake and Great-Aunt Cloris at least would be dressing for supper. Eugenia must be present when she came downstairs or she would wonder why.

Her ears pricked up at the sound of the door under the porch steps opening. Eugenia peered over the railing to see Bridget emerge from the scullery. The maid was carrying a bucket of slops to the bin. She looked up in surprise as Eugenia unlatched the gate and hurried down the steps.

"Where did you come from, miss?" asked Bridget.

"I – went out for – for a stroll," replied Eugenia.

Bridget's eyes grew wide with interest. "Alone, miss?"

"Yes," asserted Eugenia, adding quickly, "you are not to tell Great-Aunt Cloris or Mama. Promise?"

Bridget looked crafty. "And what do I get if I do *promise*, miss?"

Eugenia, about to enter the scullery, paused. "*Bridget*! You want a bribe?"

"I wouldn't call it that, miss. I'd call it a *sweetener*."

Eugenia looked helpless. "But – I don't own anything you could possibly want, Bridget. And I don't have any money."

Bridget pursed her lips. She knew this was perfectly true.

"How about if you owe me, miss?"

"Owe you?"

"Yes. You might have money *one* day."

"Well – " mused Eugenia. "I cannot imagine that I am ever going to have any money, Bridget, but – all right. I agree."

"That's settled then."

Eugenia stared at her for a moment and then hurried in. She walked through the scullery to the kitchen and there made for the door which led into the corridor.

Bridget followed at her heels.

"Your great-aunt had a visitor this evening," she said.

"Who was it?"

"A Lady Biscuit or something," answered Bridget with a shrug. "She didn't stay long."

Since Bridget had nothing more to add, Eugenia opened the door and climbed up the stairs to the entrance hall. Here she removed her coat and hat. Just in time! As the supper gong sounded, Great-Aunt Cloris opened her drawing room door.

"Ah! Eugeeeenia. Have you been asleep? The house was very quiet all afternoon."

Eugenia could not meet her narrowed eye.

"Y-yes, great-aunt. I was asleep."

She nodded. "Well. You missed a visit from an old friend of mine. No matter. Let us go in to supper. Needless to say, your mother will not be joining us!"

Great-Aunt Cloris was uncharacteristically garrulous over the fish supper. Eugenia barely listened. She prodded at her meal listlessly, her mind on the unfortunate encounter with the Marquis.

It was very – *gallant* of him to come to her rescue, she supposed, but what must he think of her, alone in the park like that? She coloured as she imagined the construction the Marquis might make of it all.

She refused to consider the fact that the Marquis had been good to her father – had indeed treated him more as a friend than as an employee. She refused to dwell on the fact that the Marquis had been kind to her when she was a little girl at her first Christmas party.

As far as she was concerned, the more decidedly she could thwart her mother's designs, the better. The unfavourable first impression she had made on the Marquis at the soirée must now be compounded by the encounter in the park. *Nothing* her mother might do or say could rectify that.

The Marquis could now be even more definitively struck from the list of her prospective suitors!

In this, Eugenia was to be proved completely wrong!

*

The visit from her friend Lady Bescombe had set Great-Aunt Cloris thinking. Lady Bescombe's portrait had recently been painted – 'for posterity'. The artist, one Gregor Brodosky, though apparently well known in his native Russia, was not yet established in England. This fact was of no concern to Great-Aunt Cloris except insofar as it meant he could not charge overmuch for his services.

Posterity had never greatly appealed to Great-Aunt Cloris. She had always suspected that it would entail a great deal of expense. The prospect of posterity *at no great cost,* however, attracted her greatly. She also became convinced that, suitably framed and hung, she would be able to keep an eye on household expenditure long after her demise.

This last idea clinched the matter. She took up her pen

and wrote to Mr. Gregor Brodosky, care of the Moskova Club, Kensington.

Eugenia and her mother were astonished when Great-Aunt Cloris announced her intention. Privately Mrs. Dovedale considered that the money might be better spent on a new wardrobe for Eugenia. She mentioned that she had heard of this artist, Brodosky, from Lady Granton, who had described him as enigmatic and devilishly handsome. He was setting many a lady's heart aflutter. Great-Aunt Cloris said she had no interest in such matters.

"I shall not be looking at *him*," she remarked imperiously. "Rather, he will be looking at *me*."

The idea of being looked at took such root in Great-Aunt Cloris, that the following morning she sent Eugenia to Bond Street Arcade to purchase some rouge and lip colour.

Eugenia undertook the task with alacrity. She enjoyed strolling through the Arcade, looking at all the pretty items in the shops.

Bridget, who accompanied her, shifted the basket on her arm and grunted.

"You'll have all them things one day, miss."

"Not I!" laughed Eugenia. "I shall marry a penniless poet!"

Wending their way home, they paused opposite Great-Aunt Cloris's house in Craven Hill to watch a handsome carriage drive by.

The carriage drove to the end of the street, where the driver sat for a minute, seeming uncertain of which way to proceed.

Eugenia and Bridget crossed the road and went into the house.

Eugenia was still in the hallway removing her gloves when the doorbell rang.

"Bridget, answer the door please."

A footman, looking very important in scarlet britches, stood on the step outside. Behind him, the carriage Eugenia and Bridget had espied a moment ago was waiting at the kerb.

"Delivery for a Mrs. and Miss Dovedale!" he announced with a bow.

Two pageboys emerged from the carriage. One staggered under a large hamper with Fortnum and Mason written on the side. The other carried a box wrapped in silver paper and tied with a pink bow.

The footman gave another bow.

"With the compliments of the Marquis of Buckbury," he said.

"What is all the commotion?" asked Great-Aunt Cloris from the landing above.

Eugenia cleared her throat.

"It is a delivery, Great-Aunt Cloris. From – from the Marquis of Buckbury."

"Marquis? Did someone mention the Marquis?" cried Mrs. Dovedale from behind Great-Aunt Cloris.

The hamper, addressed to Mrs. Dovedale, contained a large ham, tinned fruit, oatmeal biscuits, a stilton, plum cake and champagne.

The box was addressed to Eugenia. From its layers of tissue she drew a jewelled fan and a pair of kid gloves.

"There is an envelope, too!" said Mrs. Dovedale excitedly. "Addressed to both of us."

The envelope contained an invitation to a ball to be given by Lord and Lady Bescombe the following month.

Mrs. Dovedale's eyes gleamed. "Lord and Lady Bescombe's *ball*. Imagine."

"No good will come of it," sniffed Great-Aunt Cloris.

Eugenia could not but silently agree.

In her room later she stared numbly at the fan and gloves.

The Marquis must surely know that she had never owned anything of such quality. Were these gifts meant to illustrate what she had lost when she first spurned his interest?

Clearly, in revenge for her initial snub, the Marquis wished to humiliate Eugenia. The encounter in the park had intensified his contempt. No doubt he had not believed her when she had said that she had not known the man who accosted her. Perhaps he thought she had declined the interest of a Marquis for the attentions of someone who was not even a gentleman.

Rich men were cruel and proud. She would have nothing to do with them.

She would write to the Marquis and refuse his invitation to the ball. She would inform her mother of her decision the very next day.

The gifts and the invitation to the ball had revived Mrs. Dovedale. For the first time in days, she rose from her bed and dressed for breakfast. She sat at table, humming so happily as she buttered her toast, that Eugenia's heart sank.

"Mama," she began with trepidation.

She waved her butter knife at her daughter. "You are worrying that you have no dress but never fear. I have decided to sell the jewellery left to me by my own mother and your dear father. I shall take the pieces to Hatton Garden tomorrow. I am bound to achieve a good price and then you and I shall go to Bond Street to purchase some material."

Eugenia swallowed hard. "Mama, you can't!"

"Oh, but I can. Your father would applaud. You *shall* go the ball, my dear!"

Eugenia sighed.

She would need to broach the subject later. Meanwhile she would write to the Marquis. She would send Bridget out, or post the letter herself while she and her mother were on their afternoon walk.

Mrs. Dovedale, however, sent down word at lunch that all the excitement had given her a headache and she wished to rest. Bridget should accompany Eugenia on her constitutional.

The air was sharp. Eugenia wore one of her aunt's old fur hats. Tucked in her muff was the letter for the Marquis. She would walk as far as Kensington Gore and post it there.

Eugenia walked swiftly – too swiftly for Bridget, who lagged sullenly behind. Eugenia's cheeks were soon rosy with exertion.

The Broad Walk, when she reached it, was busy. Ladies strolled arm in arm, boys bowled hoops or chased each other up and down, open carriages drove by at a sedate pace.

"Miss Dovedale!"

Eugenia looked up as one such carriage drew close. She paled when she recognised the Marquis of Buckbury.

"My Lord!"

The Marquis called to his driver, who brought the vehicle to a halt. Eugenia dropped a curtsy as the Marquis stepped out.

"How delightful to encounter you, Miss Dovedale. Might I walk with you a little?"

The Marquis spoke in so civil a tone that Eugenia did not know how to refuse.

"If – if you so wish," she stammered.

The Marquis gestured to his driver to follow and then he and Eugenia set off at a stroll.

"It's a fine day to be out, Miss Dovedale."

"Yes, it is, my Lord."

"I trust your mother is well?"

"She is – indisposed today."

"I am sorry to hear that."

"But I am not alone, all the same – you see – there is Bridget behind."

The Marquis turned gravely to acknowledge the presence of Bridget. Then he and Eugenia continued to walk in silence.

'*He is waiting for me to thank him for his gifts*!' Eugenia thought.

She knew she should thank him there and then, but she felt as if the words would stick in her throat. The truth was, in her heart, that she did not thank him at all! Yet the longer she remained silent, the more difficult it would be to broach the subject.

She drew to a sudden halt and stood with lowered eyes, tracing a line in the gravel of the Broad Walk with the toe of her boot. Bridget, some ten paces behind, flopped down thankfully onto a bench and yawned. The Marquis, puzzled, stopped as well.

"I – have a letter for you – in my muff," ventured Eugenia at last.

The Marquis raised an eyebrow. "In your muff?"

Eugenia looked up. "Yes. It – it thanks you for your gifts – "

The Marquis bowed.

"But – "

He waited.

"But?" he prompted.

Eugenia faltered. "P-perhaps you should read it." She withdrew the letter from her muff and held it out.

31

The Marquis took the letter and opened it. He read in silence.

"You put it most succinctly," he said when he had finished. "You neither sought nor welcomed my gifts – "

Eugenia nodded.

" – and you do not wish to accept my invitation to Lady Bescombe's ball."

Eugenia bit her lip and nodded again.

"Miss Dovedale," he said, "I understand that I may have in some way offended your pride. In my defence, I should explain that I simply wished to help the family of a gentleman for whom I felt both affection and respect."

Eugenia felt uncomfortable. This was not how she had imagined the Marquis would respond.

"You – are speaking most kindly – considering that I have been – rather rude," she murmured in a low voice.

"Rude?"

"At Lady Granton's – I commented on – "

She could not finish.

The corner of the Marquis's lips twitched. "The fact that I – was of a greater age than when we last met?"

Eugenia dropped her head. "Yes."

"My dear Miss Dovedale, I must admit I was nonplussed at your remark, but it did not take long for me to see that I should attribute it to the – inexperience of tender youth. A youth," he added with a slight smile, "so far behind me it is almost a mystery!"

The vein of humour caught Eugenia off guard.

Well," she whispered. "I am sorry all the same."

"No more of that then," said the Marquis brusquely. "Now. May I hope that you will reconsider the invitation to the ball?"

Eugenia's head shot up. "That's not possible! Mama would have to sell her jewellery and – oh!"

Her hand flew to her mouth as she realised what she had divulged.

The Marquis was frowning. "Sell her jewellery?"

"No, no, I should not have said it! Mama would be so distressed – "

"I shall say nothing, Miss Dovedale. But you do realise – this now makes two secrets that we share?"

The Marquis's tone was teasing but this did not reassure Eugenia. Reminded of the recent unpleasant encounter in the gardens she became agitated. The Marquis knew too much about her altogether!

Her fingers closed nervously over each other in her muff.

"You will excuse me now, my Lord. I must return and see how my mother is faring."

"Miss Dovedale, my carriage is at your disposal."

"Thank you, I shall walk."

"May I call on you and your mother tomorrow?"

Eugenia dreaded her mother using such a visit to further entertain notions of a romance between her daughter and the Marquis. Yet she did not feel it proper to decline on her mother's behalf.

"I suppose – you may," she replied.

She turned towards home. Bridget sprang to her feet and trotted after her.

Eugenia was puzzled by the Marquis. He seemed genuinely interested in the fortunes of herself and her mother. Perhaps he really did want to help them. On the other hand, he had wealth and that meant he had power. People enjoyed power and often used it to entertain themselves. Perhaps having power over his late High

Steward's family gave him pleasure.

'Well, I shall not allow him to have power over *me*,' Eugenia decided.

Reaching home, she threw off her coat and hat in the hall and bounded up the stairs, anxious to check on her mother. Bridget picked up the coat and scowled after her.

Mrs. Dovedale was not in her room. Perhaps, feeling better, she had gone to see Great-Aunt Cloris.

Eugenia hurried towards the next flight of stairs.

Half-way up, a piercing whistle startled her. Hand on the banister, she halted and raised her head.

A young man stared down at her from the landing above.

Eugenia felt her heart lurch in her breast.

The eyes that surveyed her were unlike any she had ever seen. Green as agate, blazingly intense, they compelled her gaze. The face in which they were set was striking with its large nose and wide cheekbones. White-blond hair flopped untidily over the young man's face and hung to his shoulders.

Tossing the hair from his brow, the young man began to descend the stairs. All the while his eyes seemed to burn into Eugenia's. Slowly and one step at a time he came, murmuring to her all the while.

"I was thinking, how can I paint here, in this old house? There is no light, no light! Everything is brown. Then you appear. You are like the sun! You bring this gold, gold hair. Is it really gold? May I touch it? I must touch it!"

Eugenia – lips parted, eyes wide – found herself nodding. This was obviously Gregor Brodosky the painter.

One step above her, he halted and plunged his fingers into her hair.

"What are these pins? They are like spears. Out, out!"

Eugenia began to tremble as Gregor tore pins from her hair and tossed them aside.

"Now. See. It falls. It is gold, melting over you. Ah, what a face! *You* I could paint! But my fate is to paint the old gorgon upstairs!"

Shocked, Eugenia pulled her head away. "Oh, you must not speak like that. Great-Aunt Cloris appears cross but underneath she is good and kind – "

Gregor roared. "She is good. She is kind. She is ugly. Never mind. Maybe I paint you later. If she will pay. Maybe I paint you anyway. She does not like to pay. But I think she is rich, all the same?"

Eugenia faltered. Was he really asking her this question. "I – don't know. I do not enquire."

"No. You do not ask. You are angel!"

Before Eugenia could protest, Gregor caught her chin in his hand and, bending his head, planted a kiss on her startled mouth. Then he let go and ran off down the stairs, whistling again. He neither looked back nor waved goodbye.

Fingers to her lips, as if to seal in Gregor's kiss, Eugenia turned and stumbled to her room.

She could not face Great-Aunt Cloris and her mother. Something had happened to her and she did not want them to know. They would be able to tell if they saw her, she was sure. Her lips must be blood-red, her cheeks full of fire.

She sank onto her bed and clasped her hands to her bosom.

At last, at last, she had met a man who was the essence of romance.

And he was surely a lover of whom her mother could never approve in a million years!

CHAPTER THREE

Mrs. Dovedale was not with Great-Aunt Cloris. She had suspected that Eugenia would oppose her selling the jewellery and so she had pretended to have a headache in order to stay behind while Eugenia and Bridget visited the park. Once they had left the house, she had snatched up her hat and coat and taken a hansom cab to Hatton Garden.

She had not received quite the amount for her jewellery that she had hoped, but it was enough. She would be able to dress Eugenia and perhaps even herself for the ball and then – and then all their problems would be solved.

Mrs. Dovedale was convinced that the Marquis was smitten with Eugenia. She was equally convinced that Eugenia would ultimately succumb to the Marquis's undoubted charms, not least of which was his ownership of Buckbury Abbey.

She returned home in the same hansom. A light rain was falling as the vehicle drew up outside Great-Aunt Cloris's house.

The following day Gregor arrived with his brushes and tubes of paint and an easel to paint Great-Aunt Cloris.

Eugenia listened eagerly to the sound of his voice as he greeted Bridget in the hallway below.

She stood inside her door, thrilling to the rhythm of his footsteps as he mounted the stairs and passed her room. He was so close to her and yet she could not see him. She *dared* not see him. She envied Bridget when later she opened her door a crack and observed the maid carrying lunch up to Great-Aunt Cloris's room.

"What are they doing?" she whispered as Bridget came down again with an empty tray.

Bridget stared at Eugenia. "Your great-aunt is sitting in a chair, miss, and the painter is – painting."

"Thank you." Eugenia sighed and closed her door again.

She would love to have watched Gregor at work. But her mother and great-aunt had obviously exchanged words on the subject for, over the next few days, Eugenia was never invited to Great-Aunt Cloris's room while the young Russian was present.

Each morning she found her heart racing as she waited for the sound of the bell. She stood inside her door, willing Gregor to raise his voice as he passed by with Bridget.

So infused with thoughts of Gregor was she that Eugenia never once thought to enquire about the jewels that her mother had decided to sell. The jewels – the Bescombe ball – the Marquis – seemed subjects from another world and time entirely.

One bright morning, she at last plucked up the courage to open her door just a fraction as Gregor and Bridget passed on their way.

She opened the door so carefully that there was not the slightest creak from the hinge and it was no surprise that Gregor did not turn his head as she peeped out at him. But as he mounted the stairway to Great-Aunt Cloris's room, he suddenly lifted his hand and gave her a backward wave.

She closed her door quickly.

When she heard him descending the stairs at the close of day, she opened her door fully and came out. He was alone. Great-Aunt Cloris had not rung for Bridget to show him out.

"I was just – going down to the parlour," Eugenia said, wondering how it was that the loud clamour of her heart was not audible.

Gregor grinned. "No, little flower. You want to see Gregor."

Eugenia gasped. "How did you know?"

Quick as a flash, Gregor caught hold of her hand and pressed it to his breast.

"What can you hear?" he asked mysteriously.

"H-hear?"

"*Boom boom. Boom boom.* A Russian heart. Very loud, no? When *you* are near, very loud! And your heart too, when I am near, very loud." Gregor threw back his head and laughed. "That is how I know! Ha ha ha. Very loud."

With that, Gregor dropped Eugenia's hand and strolled on down the stairs,whistling.

Eugenia stared after him in wonder.

She had never met anyone like him. There *was* no one like him, not in London, not in England, not in the whole wide world.

And he had said that his heart beat extra loudly when *she,* Eugenia, was near!

The next day was Saturday. She paced her room, waiting for the doorbell to ring. The hall clock chimed ten. He was usually here by now. Ten thirty. Eleven.

Her heart sank. Obviously he did not work on a Saturday.

Her week had been so taken up with waiting to hear Gregor's voice, waiting to catch a glimpse of him, that a break in this routine left her feeling beached on some grey and deserted island.

At last she ambled to the dark old library at the back of the house. She needed a book to take her mind off the long, desolate weekend that lay ahead.

Her great-aunt's late husband, Mr. Dewitt, had been interested in cloth, trade, the distillation of whiskey and little else. It was some time before Eugenia found anything that might absorb her – a biography of Peter the Great. She tucked the book under her arm and left the library.

Bridget was hovering in the hallway.

"Oh, miss, I've been looking for you everywhere. You're wanted in the drawing room. There's a visitor."

Eugenia knitted her brow. "A visitor? I never heard the bell."

"No, miss. You wouldn't in there. That door is covered with baize."

Eugenia did not dare ask who the visitor might be, but her fancy ran ahead of her. Surely it was Gregor, on his day off, invited to take tea in the drawing room at the end of his first week of painting Great-Aunt Cloris's portrait!

Her mother and great-aunt looked up from the tea table as she entered. "Ah, here's Eugeeenia." Eugenia's eyes flew round the room. A figure at the window turned and smiled a welcome.

The Marquis! Eugenia's face was such a picture of disappointment that the Marquis himself could not but notice. The smile faded from his lips and his eyes hooded over.

"I am afraid Miss Dovedale was expecting someone else," he said stiffly.

"Someone else?" cried Mrs. Dovedale in alarm. "There is nobody else! We are closeted like nuns here."

Great-Aunt Cloris grunted in surprise but said nothing.

Eugenia, aware that she had revealed her emotions in a manner that was both discourteous and a little dangerous, summoned up a rush of gaiety.

"It's true!" she cried. "We eat, sleep and pray to the chime of the clock as if it was a convent bell. It is a mercy that I am not forced to wear a habit!"

The Marquis's profile seemed unyielding. "Like nuns?" he repeated.

Eugenia raised her face staunchly to his. "Yes."

"Well, I am sure that you would make even a habit look the height of fashion, Miss Dovedale."

Eugenia, regarding him closely for the first time, thought she detected a twinkle in the corner of his eye.

"Thank you," she muttered, somewhat chastened.

Mrs. Dovedale, who had been listening anxiously to this exchange, detected the easing of tension.

"Do come and have some tea," she suggested with relief.

Eugenia and the Marquis moved together to the table.

To Mrs. Dovedale, it was as if he was committing to memory every flicker of her daughter's lashes and every glance of her eye.

She could almost hear the wedding bells ringing in her head!

She gave a little cough as she poured the tea. "I am sure plans are proceeding apace for Lady Bescombe's ball?"

The Marquis dutifully tore his gaze away from Eugenia. "Indeed. I believe Lord and Lady Bescombe have hired a Viennese orchestra."

"And Italian pastry cooks," interposed Great-Aunt Cloris. "Why a plain old English baker will not do, I cannot imagine."

The Marquis's eyes had already strayed back to Eugenia. Her hair gleamed in a halo of light from the window.

"Might I hope that Miss Dovedale has changed her mind with regard to the ball?" he asked her softly. "Might I hope that she will now accept my invitation?"

Eugenia stared into her teacup. "I-I am afraid I remain quite resolute. I shall not accept."

"She jests," cried Mrs. Dovedale in horror. "She would love nothing more."

"Mama," said Eugenia sharply. "I should hope to be allowed to know for myself what I would love or not love."

The Marquis, his regard flicking from mother to daughter, felt that painful matters were about to be broached. His presence must only increase any discomfort for Eugenia. He rose graciously from the table with a bow.

"Ladies, I must beg permission to leave. I have – urgent business to attend to."

Mrs. Dovedale threw an angry glance at Eugenia before replying.

"You will call on us again? I am sure you are always very welcome."

"Thank you," replied the Marquis.

Mrs. Dovedale insisted on showing the Marquis out herself. She wanted to reassure him that she would do everything in her power to ensure that Eugenia attended the ball.

As the door closed behind them, Great-Aunt Cloris folded her hands into her lap and stared at Eugenia.

"I have half a mind to take your place at the Bescombe ball, if you won't go," she mused.

Eugenia was amazed. "But, great-aunt, you do not like such events."

"No. But Lady Bescombe is going to exhibit the portrait that Gregor painted of her at the ball. I should like to see *that*! And that is the only place I *can* see it, for she intends to send it down to her country house after the ball. And I shall never go there. Nasty, damp place."

"Gregor – painted Lady Bescombe?"

"Indeed. You may remember that it was Lady Bescombe who recommended him. You would think he was the son of Peter the Great himself, the way she treats him."

"You think – Gregor will be at the – at the ball?" Eugenia asked in a low voice.

"Undoubtedly. I shouldn't wonder if he dances with Lady Bescombe herself."

Eugenia rose trembling from her seat. "Excuse me, Great-Aunt Cloris. I have to – I have to – speak to the Marquis before he departs."

"Hmph! Everyone is deserting me now," she grumbled, but she waved her great-niece away.

Eugenia flew from the room. The hallway was empty. She glimpsed her mother at the front door, waving jauntily. She heard the sound of a carriage drawing away from the house. The Marquis had left. No matter. She would write to him.

She hurried up the stairs and into her bedroom. In the desk she found a sheet of headed notepaper. She dipped her pen into the inkwell and wrote quickly. She waved the letter in the air until the ink was dry and then she sealed it.

She had accepted the Marquis's invitation. She would go to the ball, she would dress in a gown of rose pink silk and she would dance with Gregor Brodosky. She would dance all night, only with him, and his Russian heart would go *boom, boom, boom* to hold her in his arms!

*

Eugenia stood waiting to be announced. The stairway that led down to the ballroom was of white marble, with a runner of thick red carpet. Below, the ballroom was already crowded and the orchestra playing. Figures in resplendent costume swirled by. But something was wrong. Each figure wore a mask. Eugenia felt her face with her fingers. She wore no mask. Would she be allowed to dance?

"Miss Eugenia Dovedale"

At the sound of her name, the various instruments of the orchestra began, one by one, to cease playing. Soon only the sound of a violin floated in the air. The dancers stopped and turned to watch Eugenia descend.

There was something wrong. At each step she took, someone in the ballroom began to laugh. Soon there was a chorus of laughter. A figure detached himself from the throng and came to the foot of the steps. His shoulders too were shaking.

"Her shoes! Look at her shoes!"

Eugenia glanced down. Her slippers were so worn that her toes peeped through. The hem of her dress was ragged and the sleeves ripped.

The laughter in the ballroom was now uproarious. Tears pricked Eugenia's eyes but she kept on walking down. Then the figure at the foot of the steps tore away his mask to reveal his identity.

It was Gregor, Gregor Brodosky, and he was laughing at Eugenia along with all the rest.

"Oh," choked Eugenia, struggling awake. "Oh."

She felt her face. It was wet with tears.

What a fool she was! The dream had told her that. How could she possibly go to the ball? She had no gown. Great-Aunt Cloris would never buy her one. It was all her own fault that she found herself in this dilemma. She had been so eager to dance with Gregor that she had entirely forgotten the state of her wardrobe.

Even as the memory of her mother's decision to sell off her jewellery surfaced in her mind, Eugenia suppressed it. She would *never* agree to a sale.

The Marquis would have received her letter of acceptance by now. She had sent it yesterday. Well, she would have to send him another, rescinding her decision.

Mrs. Dovedale bustled in, humming happily. Eugenia shrank in her chair. She had told her mother last night that she had accepted the invitation to the ball. She had been ecstatic but Eugenia, fearful her mother might pry into the *reason* for her change of heart, had slipped quickly away to bed. Now she would have to explain yet another change of heart!

Her mother sat down and rubbed her hands together. "What fun we are going to have these next few days, Eugenia my dear."

"Fun?" echoed Eugenia faintly.

"Preparing for the ball, dear."

"Mama," she said quietly. "There isn't going to be any fun. You see, I-I have changed my mind. I am – not going to the ball after all."

Mrs. Dovedale spluttered. "Not going?"

"No."

"You tiresome girl! What do you mean by this incessant torment of your mother?"

"Mama," pleaded Eugenia. "I cannot go. I have no dress. I will not go in any more hand-me-downs."

"Oh, is that it?" Mrs. Dovedale looked as if she would faint with relief. "You do not have to worry about that. Everything is arranged."

"Arranged?"

"I now have the money." Her mother looked triumphant. "Tomorrow we will go and choose the material and then hire a dressmaker. She will have to work quickly. It is only a week to the ball."

Eugenia paled. "How do you have the money? Have you sold your jewellery? I will absolutely refuse to see a dressmaker if you have sold your jewellery! And if I find out afterwards, I will never, never forgive you!"

Mrs. Dovedale hesitated. Her daughter's expression was so resolute that she could not doubt that Eugenia had meant what she said.

"N-no, dear," she replied slowly. "I have not sold the jewellery."

Mrs. Dovedale pondered all through breakfast. She remained in the parlour after Eugenia went up to dress. When Bridget came in to clear the table she asked the maid to bring her a pen and paper. She wanted to write a letter and it was warmer in the parlour than in her bedroom.

Bridget complied with Mrs. Dovedale's request. She wrote slowly, considering every word. Then she sealed the letter and handed it to Bridget.

"You are to take this directly to the address you see on the envelope. I shall give you a shilling for a hansom cab. And," she added, "you must on no account tell Miss Eugenia."

*

Sunday seemed long and tedious to Eugenia. Her mother made no further reference to the ball or indeed to the question of money and she, for all her suspicions, was happy to avoid the subject for the moment.

So eager was she to attend the ball now she knew that Gregor would be there that she did not wish to speculate too keenly on where money might have come from. As long as it was not from the sale of her mother's jewellery! Perhaps Great-Aunt Cloris had somehow been prevailed upon to pay for new gowns. No doubt the old lady would let her know soon enough.

After returning from Church the weather became

inclement, which meant there would be no walk that afternoon. Instead, Mrs. Dovedale asked Eugenia to come to her room to read to her. Eugenia scanned the room for sight of the jewellery box and was relieved to see that it sat undisturbed in its usual place. When her mother seemed asleep, Eugenia tiptoed over to the box and, lifting it, gave it a little shake. It was locked so she could not be sure, but it seemed full. Satisfied, she set it down again.

Her mother stifled a smile in her pillow, thankful that she had thought to fill the box with loose buttons and bobbins of cotton.

All she required now was a positive response to the letter she had written earlier that day –

Reassured that her mother had indeed not sold her jewellery, Eugenia felt free to daydream again of the ball and the dances she would share with Gregor Brodosky.

The following morning she put a tortoiseshell comb in her hair. Every few minutes she ran to the mirror to pinch her cheeks. She must keep them looking rosy for Gregor.

At ten o'clock she heard a carriage draw up outside. Her heart quickened. Perhaps Gregor had decided not to walk to the house this morning. It was still raining, after all.

The doorbell sounded. She waited, heart pounding, but nobody ascended the stairs. Puzzled, she opened the door and walked out on to the landing.

The Marquis and her mother stood in the hallway below, talking in low voices. As Eugenia watched the Marquis drew a large packet from his overcoat. He handed it to Mrs. Dovedale. She appeared to thank him and then ushered him into the drawing room.

Eugenia frowned. What was the Marquis doing here, so early in the day? She hoped she was not going to be summoned to take tea with him. She might miss the arrival of Gregor.

At ten thirty the bell sounded again. This time it *must* be Gregor! She heard voices, louder than before and stepped out onto the landing. The Marquis was on the point of leaving and had stopped to exchange greetings with Gregor. Drawing on his gloves as he spoke, he glanced up over Gregor's head and saw Eugenia gazing down.

She flushed under his stare and drew back. The Marquis departed. Gregor waved Bridget away – she was preparing to escort him to Great-Aunt Cloris's room – and bounded up the stairs, two steps at a time. Eugenia stepped out again from the shadows.

"Ha! Little flower," he said.

"Gregor – " Eugenia flushed again at the sound of his name so openly on her lips. "Gregor – did you know that – I too am going to the ball?"

"At the Lady Bescombe's house?"

"Yes. Will you – will you dance with me there?"

"Every dance that is not promised to another, I will dance!"

Eugenia blenched. "Are there many you have promised – to others?"

A strange look crossed Gregor's features. "You are questioning me?" he growled.

"No." Eugenia was non-plussed. "No. Why do you use that tone?"

Gregor regarded her darkly from under a lank of hair. Then suddenly he tossed his head and grinned.

"What a delicate creature! How the wolves would gobble you up?"

"W-wolves?"

"In Russia, there are wolves." Gregor came close. Eugenia trembled as she felt his breath on her cheek. "They eat young girls. Like this."

His mouth touched her face. Her lip, her nose, her chin. Then he drew away laughing. "We will dance. Never fear." he cried, and ran on up to Great-Aunt Cloris.

Eugenia, stunned, gazed after him.

She could not fathom his character, but what did that matter? He was surely the most exciting man she was ever going to meet!

A little later she was summoned to her mother's room.

Eugenia could not help noticing the jewellery box on the bedside cabinet. It was ostentatiously open, revealing all the jewellery that Mrs. Dovedale had once threatened to sell.

Before Eugenia could ask, her mother ventured the information that the Marquis had called earlier to offer them the use of one of his carriages for the ball.

Eugenia thought she would enjoy driving to Lady Bescombe's in a beautiful carriage, even if it did belong to the Marquis. She refrained from expressing her enthusiasm, however. She was painfully aware of the inference her mother already drew from the fact that Eugenia had agreed to go to the ball. She told herself it was not her fault if her mother imagined romance where romance there was none.

She wondered aloud about the packet, however. Mrs. Dovedale had not realised that Eugenia had witnessed the exchange and looked somewhat disconcerted. She plucked at a loose thread on her cuff for a moment before replying.

"The Marquis had brought me some herbal remedy for recurring headaches," she said.

Before Eugenia could pursue the subject her mother hurried on.

The Marquis had, it appeared, also come to recommend a particular dressmaker in the Burlington Arcade, a Madame Lefain. Many ladies of his acquaintance had their gowns made by her.

As intended, this item of information distracted Eugenia. She asked eagerly when she and her mother might visit the dressmaker and was told that they would leave that very minute.

Eugenia hurried away to don her hat and coat.

Madame Lefain stocked a large range of materials in premises behind the Arcade. There was silk and silk mousseline and taffeta and crepe and muslin and satin and satin brocade, in a hundred colours. Eugenia's eyes opened in wonder at the choice. How could she possibly decide? She might have been there all afternoon had her gaze not alighted on a bolt of rose pink satin. This was the colour she had imagined when she had envisaged herself dancing with Gregor.

Madame Lefain thought the rose pink an excellent choice. She showed Eugenia a pattern that she thought would be most becoming and was absolutely '*of ze moment*'.

Mrs. Dovedale chose a deep purple indigo silk.

Shoes were produced that Madame Lefain assured them she could have been dyed to match the gowns.

Mrs. Dovedale declared herself most satisfied with the purchases. Eugenia tried to appear non-committal but inside she was excited beyond measure. Not since she was a child at '*Paragon*' had she been able to spend time and money on her appearance.

If she dazzled Gregor it would be more than worth it.

*

The day of the final fitting came. Madame Lefain fussed about Eugenia, straightening the hem here, shifting the shoulder there. Then at last she stepped back.

"*Voila!*"

Eugenia blinked at her image in the pier glass. Could that – *Princess* – really be her?

Mrs. Dovedale clapped her hands. "Splendid! You must go and show yourself to Great-Aunt Cloris."

"Oh, yes!" agreed Eugenia. "Since it is all her doing!"

Mrs. Dovedale caught her daughter's arm. "All her doing?"

"Did she not agree to pay for our gowns?"

Her mother hesitated. "Of course. But you must not mention it. She wishes it to be – an anonymous gift. So please do not take it upon yourself to thank her."

Eugenia was surprised but nodded all the same. "All right. If that is her wish, I shall say nothing."

It was a Saturday. Mounting the stairs to her great-aunt's room Eugenia found herself grateful for the first time that Gregor would *not* be there. She did not want to spoil his first sight of her at Lady Bescombe's ball.

Great-Aunt Cloris seemed moved when she saw how beautiful her great-niece looked. She moved stiffly to her dressing table and took out a row of pearls that had a pink lustre to them.

"You must wear these. They will go very well with the dress."

"Oh, thank you, Great-Aunt Cloris. They are perfect."

The evening of the ball arrived at last. At seven o'clock a carriage bearing the Buckbury crest arrived at the door. Great-Aunt Cloris and Bridget watched from the house as the footman opened the carriage door and ushered Eugenia and her mother inside. They waved and the carriage set off.

Mrs. Dovedale was barely settled into the plush velvet interior than she was at the window, opening it to see who might be watching their grand progress through the streets.

"Why, no one is out to notice us at all!" she moaned. She thought for a moment and then called to the coachman.

"Could you endeavour to drive by Cavendish Square, my man? And be sure and stop at Lady Granton's house at number 32."

"What are you asking, Mama?" whispered Eugenia.

"Lady Granton is not attending the ball tonight," her mother replied. She is somewhat unwell. I should like her to see us in our gowns."

Eugenia shook her head and leaned back against the soft upholstery.

The coachman, in order to detour by Cavendish Square, was turning the carriage round at a crossroads. Mrs. Dovedale hung out at the window, calling out instructions.

"You need to turn that horse's head a little more firmly. And aim for that street on the left."

There was a shout of warning. Horses reared whinnying in their shafts. Wheels grated against wheels. The Buckbury carriage shuddered on its axle.

Eugenia started up in horror as the door against which her mother was leaning swung wildly open and she was flung out, screaming, into the dark and misty night.

There was a thud and the screaming ceased.

Trembling, Eugenia leapt from the carriage.

"Mama! Mama!"

There was no reply.

Mrs. Dovedale lay silent, unmoving, her purple gown spread wide on the cobbles, her feet in their satin shoes protruding at an odd angle. Way above her head a jet flame fluttered in its bowl like a lone moth lost in the darkness.

CHAPTER FOUR

"I knew no good would come of the ball," muttered Great-Aunt Cloris.

Eugenia shuddered. Her eye strayed to the lamp on the table behind Great-Aunt Cloris. The wick was low, the flame flickering.

Flickering. Fluttering. Like the gas jets of the street lamps when her mother lay injured on the cobbles below.

Eugenia covered her face with her hands.

It was all her fault!

If she had not wanted to dance with Gregor – if she had remained true to her original resolution not to attend the ball – she and her mother would never have been riding in that carriage. Her mother would be safe and sound, instead of lying unconscious in her bed upstairs.

People had flocked to help after the accident. The footman, the coachman and another gentleman had carried Mrs. Dovedale back into the carriage. The carriage was not too badly damaged and was able to convey the injured woman and her daughter home to Craven Hill. The coachman had then driven on to inform the Marquis that his guests would not be arriving after all.

Bridget had been sent to fetch the doctor.

Doctor Parfitt had been with Mrs. Dovedale for over half an hour. His footsteps were audible as he moved about the room upstairs.

Great-Aunt Cloris raised her eyes to the ceiling.

"That doctor has a heavy tread," she grumbled. "A heavy fee, too, I shouldn't wonder."

Eugenia lowered her head.

There was silence for a while, broken only by the snap of a log in the fireplace or the step of the doctor in the room above. Outside in the street came the sound of a carriage drawing up but neither Eugenia nor Great-Aunt Cloris stirred. Only when the door bell rang did they look up.

"A visitor at this hour?" Great-Aunt Cloris frowned.

Bridget's light footsteps sounded in the hallway. They heard the opening of the street door, muffled voices and then steps approaching the drawing room door.

"The Marquis of Buckbury," Bridget announced grandly.

Eugenia rose in confusion as the Marquis strode forward, pulling off his long gloves. Raindrops glistened in his hair and the collar of his dark cape was damp.

"You – you have left the ball before it was hardly begun, my Lord?" Eugenia murmured.

"Did you really think I could simply dance the night away after hearing the terrible news?" The Marquis shook his head wonderingly before turning to address Great-Aunt Cloris. "I have taken the liberty, ma'am, of ordering straw to be laid outside your house that the invalid might not be disturbed by the sound of traffic."

"How kind of you to think of such a thing, my Lord." She signalled to Bridget, who stood gaping at the door. "Bridget, take our visitor's cape to dry. Then be so good as to bring us some tea."

Eugenia meanwhile bestirred herself to bring a chair to the fire for the Marquis.

"The doctor is with Mrs. Dovedale now?" he enquired.

"This last half hour," replied Great-Aunt Cloris. "We await his prognosis – with great trepidation, as you might imagine. My niece was as cold as a waxwork when they brought her home. She has not opened her eyes nor uttered a word since."

The Marquis listened with concern. He then turned to Eugenia.

"You were not in any way – injured yourself, Miss Dovedale?"

"Not at all." Eugenia's voice trembled. "But Mama – poor Mama!

She turned away to stifle a sob. Only Great-Aunt Cloris registered the look of relief that crossed the Marquis's features at this admission that Eugenia was unharmed. He stood for a moment regarding her bowed head and then placed his hand gently on her arm.

"Everything that can possibly be done for your mother will be done, Miss Dovedale," he assured her.

Great-Aunt Cloris looked alarmed. "We have to hope that Mrs. Dovedale's injuries are not grave. She might be my own flesh and blood, but *I* cannot afford to pay in perpetuity for the services of a doctor. My husband's money was in Indian cotton, my Lord, and the market is not as healthy as it once was."

"Great-Aunt Cloris – please do not fret yourself," said Eugenia in a low voice. "I will pay for the doctor if – if Mama – is badly injured. I will find work somewhere."

She snorted. "What work could a young girl like you possibly do?"

Eugenia reddened, conscious of the presence of the Marquis.

"I could be a seamstress. Or governess."

Great-Aunt Cloris threw up her hands. "A seamstress! A governess! There has never been such employ in the history of the Dewitt family!"

Eugenia's lip trembled. "Begging your pardon, great-aunt, but I am not a Dewitt. I am a Dovedale."

The Marquis noted this display of spirit with interest.

"A Dovedale, ay, more's the pity!" asserted Great-Aunt Cloris sourly. "My niece Florence *could* have married a Dewitt cousin. She would not have found herself in such penury if she had. The Dewitts knew about money. *Earn it, save it.* That was their motto and it served them well."

The Marquis gave a cough. "If your niece *had* married her cousin, madam," he smiled, "the union might not have resulted in such a such a beautiful and devoted young lady as Miss Dovedale."

Great-Aunt Cloris shrugged. Then, though she struggled against it, the glare in her eye softened.

"I daresay. Yes. Eugenia is a good girl and a pretty girl. A ray of sunshine in my old age."

The following moment of delicate silence was punctured only by the arrival of Bridget. She plunged breathlessly through the door without a tray of tea.

"The doctor – is on his way, ma'am," she stuttered.

The doctor was still rolling his sleeves down as he entered the room.

Great-Aunt Cloris stood and steadied herself on the arm of her chair.

"Well?" she asked.

Doctor Parfitt tightened the button on his left cuff. "She is conscious, madam."

"Thank God! And is she – *compos mentis*? She fell headfirst into the roadway, you know! I had feared a broken skull."

"There is no sign of serious head injury. However, she is in shock and some degree of pain. She has sustained a broken leg and a fractured wrist."

Eugenia's hands flew to her mouth. "Oh! Poor Mama! Can I see her?"

The doctor considered and then gave a nod. "I am sure it will hearten her to see you. But I must insist on accompanying you. She is still very weak."

"I must come too!" insisted Great-Aunt Cloris.

The doctor turned to stay her – unwilling as he was to see his patient crowded, but Great-Aunt Cloris brushed him imperiously aside.

"Marquis! You should come too," she called over her shoulder.

The Marquis drew back. "I hardly think – " he began, but Great-Aunt Cloris cut him short.

"Mrs. Dovedale will be delighted to know that you have taken an interest in her recovery. She will wish to thank you herself."

Thus it was that the Marquis followed Great-Aunt Cloris, the doctor and Eugenia up the stairs to see Mrs. Dovedale.

Mrs. Dovedale lay propped up on pillows. Eugenia almost wept to see how pale and weak she looked.

Her eyelids fluttered open. "Is that you, daughter?"

"Yes, Mama. Great-Aunt Cloris is here too. And – and the Marquis."

"The Marquis!" Mrs. Dovedale's other hand flew to her face. "But my hair is loose and – the powder is gone from my cheeks."

Great-Aunt Cloris peered round the curtains. "I am glad to see that you are in one piece, Florence. You will be up and about in no time."

Mrs. Dovedale's eyelids fluttered in distress. "Up and about!" she moaned. "I can barely move. I haven't an ounce of strength in my bones."

"Dear, dear," said Great-Aunt Cloris, looking most perturbed. "How long do you expect to remain – prone?"

The doctor stepped forward. "Mrs. Dovedale is going to need some time to recuperate."

"Time?" echoed Great-Aunt Cloris weakly.

"One cannot be exact," the doctor began, but she cut him short.

"Who is to nurse her?" she wailed. "I cannot pay for a nurse, you know."

"Why, I shall nurse my mother," offered Eugenia quickly.

"Bless you, dear," murmured Mrs. Dovedale.

"But who then will look after *me*?" cried Great-Aunt Cloris, her face growing very red and strained. "Who will act as housekeeper? I cannot afford to hire a temporary house-keeper *and* provide for the upkeep of an invalid. This was not – in the scheme of things. What am I to do?"

Doctor Parfitt was regarding her closely and frowned.

"Mrs. Dewitt, you must calm yourself. Remember your blood pressure."

"My blood pressure – yes – there is a kind of mist before my eyes. I need to sit down. If you would be so kind as to escort me downstairs, doctor. I seem to remember Bridget brought in some tea. May I take your arm?"

"By all means."

The door had barely closed behind them when Eugenia, still kneeling at the bedside, burst into tears.

"Oh, Mama! How could Great-Aunt Cloris be so – so mean spirited!"

Mrs. Dovedale raised a shaking hand to stroke

Eugenia's head. "There, there," she coaxed in a feeble voice. "Don't mind your great-aunt. It's her age."

Eugenia buried her head in her arms.

"Miss Dovedale."

The voice of the Marquis rang from the shadows. Eugenia raised her tear-streaked face, having almost forgotten that the Marquis was present. She wiped her eyes with the back of her hand as the Marquis stepped into the lamplight. He reached down and helped Eugenia to her feet.

"Your mother is quite right," he said gently. "Mrs. Dewitt is elderly and elderly people can be easily frightened by any rupture in routine. She is afraid of the spectacle of injury, because it reminds her of her own increasing fragility."

"She is afraid of the expense, too!" lamented Mrs. Dovedale, clutching the sheet to her chin. "She thinks I will empty her coffers for her. Oh, if only my dear daughter and myself were not so impoverished!"

"Mama!" murmured Eugenia, mortified, but nothing would silence her once she had started on this particular topic.

"Lord knows why she is so penny-pinching," she moaned. "She has plenty of money in the bank, and hundreds of pounds tucked away in old stockings and pillowcases and frayed slippers." She eyed the Marquis craftily over the top of the sheet. "While we – myself and my poor daughter – live on little more than bread and dripping and a ration of sugar half the time."

"*Mama!*" Eugenia groaned, hiding her face in her hands.

The Marquis's lips twitched with amusement. He cleared his throat before speaking.

"Mrs. Dovedale," he said, "I have a proposal to make. I should like to put Buckbury Abbey at the disposal of you and your daughter. It is an ideal spot for you to recuperate. My own doctor will attend you. I shall not be there myself – at least not for a while – but my servants will look after you. You shall want for nothing – including bread and dripping should you so choose."

Mrs. Dovedale's eyes lit up. "Buckbury Abbey? Oh, there is nothing I could desire more. This is *most* kind of you, my Lord. Is it not, Eugenia?"

Eugenia could only give a faint nod of assent, so seized was she with a tempest of emotions.

Who knew how long it would take her mother to recover? Weeks, months? Months more likely! Months during which she, Eugenia, would not be able to so much as glimpse Gregor.

That was obviously to be her penance. It was her passion for Gregor that had caused her to change her mind and accept the invitation to the ball and that had led to the accident! But oh, how the idea of being so far away from the object of her deepest desire pained her. Yet – yet she would not be just *any*where. She would be at Buckbury Abbey.

But, she reminded herself in her next breath, *that is the home of the Marquis*, the man whose attentions she was trying to avoid.

She dreaded to ponder what interpretation her mother must already be making of his latest offer.

Beneath and beyond all these conflicting and disturbing thoughts, a faint excitement stirred.

This was related not to Buckbury, but to the little house that stood on its vast estate. The place she had loved as a child and that even now she thought of as her real home.

'*Paragon*', the Eden she had, eight years ago, so cruelly lost!

*

Great-Aunt Cloris was shocked and somewhat

ashamed of herself when she learned that the Marquis had offered sanctuary to her niece and great-niece.

Bridget meanwhile seemed almost cheerful that Mrs. Dovedale and her daughter were going away.

"You might not be home before Christmas, miss," she said with a certain glee the following morning, as Eugenia arrived in the kitchen with a basket of darning.

Eugenia stared.

Bridget had always been comely but was considered careless of her appearance, her hair pinned up anyhow and the hems of her dresses often down. Recently however she had started to take greater care. She tucked pretty combs or the odd flower in her tangled mass of black curls.

"Do you have a – a young man these days, Bridget?" Eugenia asked.

"Not me, miss. Whenever would I find the time?" Bridget giggled, but the faint flush on her neck was unmistakable.

Eugenia had no time to puzzle over Bridget, however. There was too much to do before she and her mother departed. Dresses and lingerie to be laundered, shoes to be soled and toiletries to be purchased.

Meanwhile Eugenia resolved to keep out of Gregor's way. She shut her ears to the sound of his voice and the sound of his tread on the stairs.

On the very morning of her departure, however, when she heard Gregor whistling on the stairs outside her room, her resolve crumbled. She flung open the door to appear before him.

He paused, gazing at her bemused.

"Ah! Treasure! You have been hiding from Gregor. And today you go!" He gestured down at the trunks piled in the hallway below.

Eugenia nodded numbly. "Yes. Will you – miss me?"

60

Gregor shrugged. "When I think of you, I will miss you."

Eugenia was downcast. "Oh."

With a sudden and inexplicable laugh, Gregor seized her hand and kissed it. "But I will dream of you, my flower. Why not?"

Then he continued on up the stairs, whistling again.

Eugenia stared after him resignedly. She had no right to expect more from this artistic and exotic man.

She returned to her room to finish the preparations for departure.

*

The journey to Rutland was difficult and somewhat painful for Mrs. Dovedale, but once ensconced at Buckbury, she was beside herself with delight. She soon decided that the accident had been worth it, since it had resulted in being once again back on the estate where she had spent her happiest years.

"And this time I am in the big house," she declared with satisfaction.

The big house! Never had there been such beds – sheets of fine linen, drapes of velvet, quilts of goose and duck feather. Never had she inhabited such rooms with mahogany wardrobes and deep plush sofas and marble fireplaces.

"We are in clover here," Mrs. Dovedale sighed. "Clover!"

Servants tiptoed about, bringing soups and sweetmeats and tea on silver trays. It was obvious that the Marquis had ordered his household to treat Mrs. Dovedale and Eugenia like Royalty. They wanted for nothing and Mrs. Dovedale's every whim was granted. Everything she demanded appeared in her room as if by magic.

Eugenia, in contrast, asked for nothing.

She could not deny that, after the Spartan conditions at Craven Hill, the luxuries of Buckbury were most seductive. She could not help basking in the comfort and warmth.

If she was honest, the largesse sometimes made her uneasy. Why was the Marquis proving so kind a friend? Was it simply out of sentimental regard for his late High Steward, Eugenia's father?

Most of the time, however, she was not thinking about the Marquis at all. Once her mother came to regard the accident that had befallen her as almost fortuitous, Eugenia felt less guilty about the role her secret passion for Gregor had played in that event. She felt free to dream of her secret love again.

As the days at Buckbury passed Eugenia was much occupied in tending to her mother. She read to her, wrote letters for her, brushed her hair and ate with her.

All in all, Eugenia had very little time to herself. This would not have grieved her were it not that for the fact that these duties prevented her doing the one thing that she longed to do. They prevented her from seeking out '*Paragon*'.

The formal gardens of Buckbury Abbey had been created in the first half of the eighteenth century. There were fountains and pools, avenues of trees and pavilions erected in hidden glades.

A great, central lawn extended from the South face of the house for over a mile, terminating in a long, serpentine stretch at the end of which stood a pavilion with a domed roof. Beyond this construction – known as the Apollo Pavilion – another lawn ran down to a river. On the other side of the river, the Buckbury estate woods began.

Eugenia often gazed longingly from her window at these woods.

Somewhere amidst those oaks and beeches stood '*Paragon*', but Eugenia never had time to explore. She was only ever able to snatch an hour or so to walk in the afternoon, when her mother took a nap. That was simply not enough time to make the return journey of the mile and a half that constituted the gardens, let alone reach the trees on the far side of the domed pavilion.

She wondered who was living at '*Paragon*' now. She wondered what had happened to her pets, Sugar the cat and Bud the pony.

Mrs. Dovedale and Eugenia had been at Buckbury for nearly a month when one afternoon there was a sudden sense of greater activity than usual about the place.

Strolling through the South gallery, she became aware that the large double doors leading to the private chambers of the Marquis were, for once, thrown wide open. In the room beyond, servants scurried about whisking white sheets from the furniture, while two maids were busy waxing the floor.

"What is happening?" Eugenia asked.

One of the two maids rose and gave a bob, cloth in hand.

"If you please, miss, the Marquis has sent word that he is at Kettering and will be here shortly."

"I had no idea," said Eugenia, startled.

"We're ever so pleased, miss."

"You are?"

"Oh, yes, miss. There never was a better Master. It's time he came home for good."

Eugenia made her way back to her room, musing on what she had learned from the maid. The Marquis was a popular Master, it seemed.

He arrived at ten o'clock. He did not care to disturb his guests but dined alone and retired by midnight.

The following morning he sent to request that he might call on Mrs. Dovedale and Eugenia. Mrs. Dovedale demanded Eugenia bring her pots of rouge and face powder to the bed. She urged her daughter to make herself more presentable, but Eugenia replied coldly that she did not consider herself to be on display.

After the Marquis had made solicitous enquiries of Mrs. Dovedale's health, he enquired of Eugenia whether she had been able to take advantage of the extensive gardens. Eugenia admitted she had barely begun to explore. She could not go far on foot, she added, as she did not like to leave her mother for too long.

The Marquis expressed surprise that she had not availed herself of one of the fine horses in the stables and suggested that she ride out with him that very afternoon. Eugenia hesitated, unwilling to commit herself to time alone with the Marquis, but Mrs. Dovedale rushed in to accept on her daughter's behalf. She had been rather worried that Eugenia was not getting enough fresh air.

Thus it was that, shortly after noon, Eugenia found herself seated upon a beautiful roan mare and ready to ride out with the Marquis.

She could not help noticing that everyone – the stable boy who brought the horses round, the footman who accompanied the Marquis and handed him his whip and the maid who was hurrying in from the herb garden with a bunch of sage – greeted their Master with undisguised affection, while the Marquis greeted all and sundry with great courtesy and respect.

Eugenia was surprised at how quickly she became re-accustomed to being in the saddle. It was as easy as breathing.

The Marquis led the way. They rode down the central avenue of gravel that dissected the grass parterres. On the last stretch of lawn before the lake, the horses were set to gallop. She had not felt so happy for weeks.

The Marquis reined in at the water and Eugenia followed suit. The horses steamed as they lowered their heads to drink.

The Marquis turned to speak to Eugenia but suddenly halted in his intention.

She looked bewitching, her eyes aglow, her cheeks flushed, her lips parted as she regained her breath. Her hair tumbled wildly about her shoulders.

The Marquis forced his gaze away.

"Is there any place in the vicinity you would care to visit?" he asked.

Eugenia took a deep breath and then pointed towards the woods.

"There," she said. "I should like to find the cottage where I used to live."

The Marquis smiled. "I would be rather curious to see it too. Let us go."

They set off again. They decided to ford the river, which was luckily still low, rather than use the old wooden bridge further upstream. On the other side of the water the horses scrambled up the bank and entered the woods. Eugenia's heart began to pound with excitement when they came upon the path that led to the cottage. Eagerly, she urged her horse into the lead.

A dim, green light prevailed beneath the trees. Boughs grew low, leaves brushed her forehead. She did not remember the path being so overhung or so overgrown.

She glimpsed white posts, some leaning, some fallen, some rotting. This should have prepared her for what was to come, but it did not. As the trees cleared she plunged joyously ahead and only at the last minute did she rein in her horse with a cry of utter dismay.

There before her stood '*Paragon*' or what remained of it.

The thatch had vanished, exposing the mouldering beams of the roof. Windows gaped, all glass gone. Shutters hung by a nail. The walls were peeled and cracked and in some places barely standing at all.

"Alas," sighed the Marquis. "The past is never as we remember it."

Eugenia, beside herself with grief and horror, swung wildly on her companion.

"It's all your fault!" she sobbed. "You stayed in France and neglected your estate. I suppose '*Paragon*' was beneath your interest. Why didn't you install new tenants? Why?"

Before the stunned Marquis could reply, Eugenia wheeled her horse around and took off at a gallop. She kept her head down as she careered through the low branches. She cleared the woods and splashed through the river, her mind in as great a turmoil as the darkening sky above. If her dreams of the past had been destroyed, she would cling all the tighter to her dreams of the future.

Whether her mother approved or not, she would marry the man she adored and never, never succumb to the attentions of a man who had allowed her beloved '*Paragon*' to fall into ruin!

CHAPTER FIVE

As Eugenia cantered past the Apollo Pavilion, a great flash of lightning lit up its copper dome. A few seconds later, a deafening thunder clap rent the air.

Eugenia's mount, a skittish creature at the best of times, gave a terrified neigh before breaking into a headlong gallop.

Although Eugenia had ridden as a child and though she had found herself fully at home in the saddle that morning, she was not an accomplished enough horsewoman to control an animal that was determined on its own course. She could do nothing but cling on, closing her eyes against the stinging lash of sudden rain and the mud that flew from under the mare's hooves.

Ahead lay the lake and an area of grey rocks.

Eugenia felt her strength ebbing, her grip faltering. Another moment and she would surely be pitched headfirst onto the rocks –

"Whoa, there, whoa!"

The Marquis, arriving at a gallop, reached for the mare's reins and tugged with all his strength. The mare's head jerked and she ran on for fifty yards or more but the Marquis and his horse kept pace. Checked at last, the mare drew to a trembling halt. The Marquis dropped her foam-flecked bridle and leapt to the ground as Eugenia, half faint, began to slip from her saddle.

"M-my Lord!"

She felt strong arms encompass her, a flutter of breath on her cheek as she was lifted and carried to shelter. Her eyelids flickered open and she was staring up at a painted wooden ceiling.

The Marquis deposited her gently onto a red lacquered seat. He wiped his brow with his sleeve and then stepped back out into the rain to tie the horses. Eugenia watched his movements dazedly. His task accomplished, the Marquis returned.

She had not yet regained her composure. Her bosom rose and fell heavily with each laboured breath and her face felt hot. Outside rain fell in a shimmering grey sheet. It felt as if she and the Marquis were marooned, cut off from the world.

"W-what place is this?" she asked.

"The Chinese pagoda," he answered shortly.

Since the light – such as it was – lay behind him, the Marquis was only visible in silhouette. Eugenia strained to read his expression.

"I must thank you, my Lord, for your timely rescue."

"I did what any man would have done in the circumstances, Miss Dovedale,"

His tone seemed cool and Eugenia felt herself blush. No doubt the Marquis had not forgiven her accusation that he had deliberately neglected '*Paragon*'. On reflection, she could not forgive herself. What had come over her, that she should have expected the Marquis to be as concerned as herself over the fate of her childhood home?

"My Lord, I must apologise for what I said – about '*Paragon*'."

"You spoke as you felt."

"There are many who would consider it a discourtesy, my Lord."

"I am not among them."

The diffidence of the Marquis unsettled Eugenia. She cast about for a means of more fully engaging his attention.

"Are those – figures I see up there on the ceiling, my Lord?"

The Marquis glanced up. "Yes. They are part of a painting that illustrates an old Chinese story."

"W-what kind of story?"

"A love story. Miss Dovedale, the storm has eased. I think we might risk riding on now."

Mutely, Eugenia rose and followed him to her horse. He lifted her to the saddle without a word and then immediately turned to untie his own mount.

The two rode in near silence back to the house. The rain had eased but not ceased and by the time Eugenia dismounted she was shivering and wet.

The Marquis ordered a maid to accompany Eugenia to her room and to help her shed her damp garments. Before Eugenia could bob a curtsy and reiterate her gratitude, the Marquis was gone, striding away down the corridor towards his library.

Once garbed in her warm dressing gown and her hair wrapped in a towel, Eugenia sought out her mother.

At the sight of her daughter, Mrs. Dovedale raised both her hands in relief.

"Thank God! I thought the lightning had fried you to a cinder!"

"I – we – found shelter, Mama." Mrs. Dovedale's eyes glimmered. "Ah! And did you find the Marquis – congenial?"

Eugenia unwound the towel from her head and shook her hair free before answering. "He was the perfect gentleman, Mama."

"I see." Mrs. Dovedale looked disappointed. Then her expression brightened as she brought out a letter from beneath her pillow. "A missive from Great-Aunt Cloris, my dear, received this morning. I do believe she is beginning to miss us."

Eugenia sat down at the dressing table and took up a brush. "What does she write, Mama?"

"Primarily, that her portrait is nearly completed."

The brush halted in mid-air.

"So – Gregor will be moving on?" Eugenia asked. She tried to sound nonchalant but her voice trembled a little.

"I suppose he will be," remarked Mrs. Dovedale, "once he has put the finishing touches to the painting."

There was a knock at the door and, at Mrs. Dovedale's invitation, the Marquis entered. He was dressed for travelling, which excited her interest. The Marquis explained that he was suddenly obliged to leave for London that very day. He had called in to say farewell.

Mrs. Dovedale noted with satisfaction that his eyes repeatedly strayed to where Eugenia sat at the dressing table. Her pleasure altered, however, when she saw that Eugenia had not turned to greet the Marquis, but was toying with the hairbrush, as if in a trance

"Eugenia!" she said sharply. "The Marquis has only been here two days and already he is deserting us again for the delights of London. What say you to that?"

Eugenia gave a start. "I – hope the delights are as – delightful as the Marquis – expects," she intoned lamely.

"Your mother jests, Miss Dovedale," claimed the Marquis, his tone neutral. "The truth is, that I have – unexpected business to attend to."

Aware of her mother's eagle eye upon her, Eugenia felt she should rally herself for a more elegant reply than her last effort. "You will be missed at Buckbury Abbey, I think," she said.

A slight shadow crossed the Marquis's face, but his reply when it came was almost jocular in tone.

"Ah, Miss Dovedale! The qualification of *I think* rather precludes you from being one of that sentimental number who might indeed miss me."

Eugenia was silent, puzzled that the Marquis's mood seemed to have altered once again in her favour, but Mrs. Dovedale plunged anxiously in.

"Oh, my Lord, we will *both* miss you, you can be sure. I cannot thank you enough for your hospitality."

The Marquis gave a bow. "You find life at Buckbury to your taste?"

"Oh, *yes*, my Lord. It is quite like coming home. We want for nothing."

"I am so pleased to hear it. Now, if there is any errand you wish to entrust to me whilst I am in London, please consider me at your service. A visit to your aunt, perhaps?"

Mrs. Dovedale clapped her hands. "That would be capital! She will soon be at such a loose end in that empty house."

The Marquis raised an eyebrow. "Soon?"

"She writes that her portrait is nearly completed. She will no longer have the distraction of Gregor and I fear that she has become rather accustomed to his company."

The Marquis's eyes rested a second on Eugenia before he replied.

"Then why not invite Mrs. Dewitt here, to Buckbury? I will order a suite prepared for her."

"You are too, too kind, my Lord! I was only saying to Eugenia that I was beginning to miss my aunt, despite her eccentricities."

The Marquis made his excuses and departed, bound for London. No sooner had the door closed behind him than Mrs. Dovedale began to berate Eugenia for what she perceived as her daughter's ill-conduct.

"You behaved as if you harboured no interest in the Marquis at all."

"Mama, I don't!"

Mrs. Dovedale threw up her hands. "You are an ungrateful and surly creature! Have you not an ounce of gratitude in your bones?"

"Of gratitude I have more than an ounce. But gratitude is not – interest. I am not nor ever shall be tempted to fall in love with the Marquis and I wish you would not persist in your notions to the contrary."

"You might be Mistress of Buckbury!" wailed Mrs. Dovedale. "I am sure of it."

"I would rather be Mistress of my own heart."

"You are beyond redemption!" cried Mrs. Dovedale. "Go away. Leave my sight immediately before I develop the fits"

Eugenia rose obligingly and walked to the door.

"Thank God I shall have my Aunt Cloris for company soon," Mrs. Dovedale muttered behind her.

A week later a letter came from Great-Aunt Cloris advising that she had accepted the kind invitation from the Marquis to visit Buckbury Abbey. A week after that, the Marquis's carriage bore the old lady up the driveway.

Great-Aunt Cloris waved royally from the carriage as it drew to a halt. Mrs. Dovedale did not wait for the footman to open the door, but hurried down to open it herself. Great-Aunt Cloris descended in great style.

After her came Bridget.

Eugenia's eyes widened at the sight.

Bridget, wearing one of Great-Aunt Cloris's old fur capes, looked about her with such a haughty eye it was as if she now considered herself elevated to the aristocracy rather than to the simple position of lady's maid.

"I don't care to bed down in the kitchen or in the attic no more," she proclaimed.

The footmen glanced at each other but Great-Aunt Cloris seemed amused rather than outraged at Bridget.

"Would you have guessed how very greatly a promotion would enlarge her sense of self?" she whispered to Mrs. Dovedale and Eugenia.

Eugenia was intrigued by Bridget's change of character. She stood at the door while Bridget inspected the room she had been assigned, which was adjacent to that of Great-Aunt Cloris. The maid's room was small but compact, with a chest of drawers and a latticed window overlooking a courtyard. Bridget bounced up and down on the bed and declared herself satisfied with the mattress.

"It's horsehair. That'll do me. And a feather pillow."

She threw off her cape and, leaning back on her elbows, kicked off her shoes. Eugenia was astonished to see that Bridget's feet were encased in fine silk stockings.

Eugenia decided that either Bridget had a secret beau or Great-Aunt Cloris was shedding an unprecedented amount of the items in her overstuffed wardrobe and tallboys. It was Bridget who decided to enlighten her.

"The stockings are yours, miss. I took them."

"Y-you took them?"

"Well, you owed me. Remember when I promised I wouldn't let on to your mother or great-aunt that you'd been out alone in Kensington Gardens and you agreed you'd owe me a – sweetener – for my silence?"

Eugenia nodded slowly. "That seems a very long time ago."

"Not so long that I'd forgotten. There was someone – who rather wanted to see me in silk stockings, so I – helped myself."

Eugenia shook her head in wonder at the maid's temerity. Bridget, feeling the subject was dealt with, kicked her heels together and gave a sigh.

"It's quiet here, isn't it miss?" she remarked. "You like it, do you?

"At Buckbury? Yes, I – I suppose I do. Though I miss London and – some of the people there."

"I'm going to miss London too. I wouldn't have come only – "

"Only what, Bridget?"

Bridget eyes narrowed. "Only I was, as you might say, ordered to."

"Oh, by Great-Aunt Cloris?"

"Gregor said he wanted to paint me, you know, once he finished Mrs. Dewitt."

Eugenia felt a pang of jealousy sweep through her. For a moment she even wished herself in the maid's shoes.

"He d-did?"

"Yes. He said I had quality."

Eugenia regarded Bridget with envious interest. She could not deny that Bridget had developed a blowsy beauty, her dark curls tumbling over a rosy face, her bosom almost opulent beneath her bodice.

"I can see how he might think so, Bridget, "she admitted in a low voice.

"You do?" Bridget regarded Eugenia for a moment, biting her lower lip. Then she seemed to make her mind up about some matter, for she abruptly sat up and leaned forward, her manner conspiratorial.

"He – he often talked about you, miss. He said he

74

wished you hadn't gone away. He wanted me to – to – "

"Yes?" Eugenia's heart was beating fast yet even so she did not fail to detect Bridget's reluctance to proceed.

"He wanted me to give you this." Bridget retrieved a piece of paper from her sleeve and thrust it at Eugenia. "There, I've done it," she said sullenly under her breath. "You please go away now, miss, as I want to change my clothes."

Wonderingly, exultantly, Eugenia floated from the maid's room. Her heart seemed to be singing under her ribs.

Bridget was an unlikely Cupid, but she had brought Eugenia the sweetest token in the whole wide world. A message from Gregor, all the more cherished for being so unexpected.

*

Barely had the household adjusted to the arrival of Great-Aunt Cloris than the Marquis himself returned to Buckbury. He promptly announced his intention to host a supper for some of the local gentry, with whom he felt he must reacquaint himself after his long absence from the County.

His guests at Buckbury found themselves happily included in the invitations.

During the next two days the Marquis was not often seen about the house. He rode out in the morning alone and was gone till dusk. Then he was ensconced in his study with various sombre looking gentlemen who arrived at Buckbury with bundles of papers. Or he was meeting with cook, discussing the menu for the forthcoming supper. He made brief visits to Mrs. Dovedale and Great-Aunt Cloris.

He acknowledged Eugenia with courtesy but was most attentive to the two older ladies, who afterwards pronounced themselves even more enchanted with him. This was lost on Eugenia, who was absorbed in her own thoughts.

The remark was not lost on Bridget, however, who was always attendant on Mrs. Dewitt and was therefore privy to the visits of the Marquis.

"I don't see how you can *not* fall in love with him, miss," she declared to Eugenia.

"Would *you* fall in love with him, Bridget?"

Bridget shrugged. "It's not for *me* to aim so high, is it, miss? I just wonder that you don't."

Eugenia stared.

Bridget was a puzzle. One minute the maid seemed deliberately to stoke Eugenia's interest in Gregor, the next she seemed unwilling to speak of the painter at all. Now here she was attempting to encourage Eugenia's interest in the Marquis.

*

The night of the supper arrived. The candles on the long mahogany table shed a golden glow. There were eleven guests in number, including Eugenia, Great-Aunt Cloris and Mrs. Dovedale.

Mrs. Dovedale was beside herself with excitement at being seated with such illustrious folk as the Duke of Fillerton and Sir Humphrey and Lady Petts.

Great-Aunt Cloris was not in the least overawed by the company, but her Spartan temperament was cruelly taunted by the opulence of the table, groaning as it was with silver and porcelain and dishes fit for a King. She was grieved to note that Mrs. Dovedale, positively revelled in the splendour.

Eugenia, she noted with satisfaction, appeared rather unimpressed by it all.

What Great-Aunt Cloris could not guess was that Eugenia was not so much unimpressed as uninvolved. Her thoughts were giddily elsewhere – with the piece of paper that had not left her person since she had received it three days ago and which even now was tucked securely into her bodice.

The words that were written on it seemed to burn her skin.

"Hello little flower. I am dreaming of you often. That pleases you, yes? When I see you I will take your hand, white as the moon, and I will kiss your palm. That also would please you, I think. My heart breaks that you are gone. Return soon to your devoted Gregor."

Eugenia imagined she could hear Gregor whispering those words into her ear. She grew quite flushed at the idea and kept her head bent over her dish, trembling lest someone should read her expression.

Although she sat on the right hand of the Marquis, she barely acknowledged his presence.

Mrs. Dovedale observed this disinterest on the part of her daughter with a frown. She was uncomfortably aware that to the left of the Marquis sat a handsome and wealthy widow by the name of Lady Walling. Lady Walling was not in the first flush of youth, but she was confident and rich and was proving *most* attentive to the Marquis.

After the ladies left the gentlemen to their cigars and port and repaired to the drawing room, Mrs. Dovedale took the occasion to once again scold Eugenia for her behaviour.

"I really cannot understand you. Do you imagine that you are the only creature in the world who is single and in search of a husband?"

"I have never supposed that, Mama."

"Then why did you allow Lady Walling to monopolise our charming host?"

Eugenia sighed. "Why will you not accept that I do not wish to be courted by the Marquis, Mama? Why?"

"How could any mother accept that her daughter is rash enough to throw away the chance of a lifetime?"

"But Mama – I do not love the Marquis."

"That is of no consequence, my dear. Unless you love someone else."

Her mother's expression was suddenly so searching that Eugenia's hand flew in consternation to her breast, as if she feared the letter secreted there had somehow become visible.

"Well?" demanded her mother.

Eugenia had no wish to deceive her outright, but neither did she wish to expose herself and Gregor to disapproval.

"How would I possibly know what love is, Mama?"

Mrs. Dovedale seemed satisfied with this and Eugenia was able to make her escape.

The supper party was pronounced a great success, but the Marquis seemed in no hurry to repeat it. Over the next few weeks he appeared increasingly preoccupied with business of his own, leaving his guests at Buckbury very much to their own devices. This in no way impaired their enjoyment of life in the great house.

Even Great-Aunt Cloris began to succumb to the hundred and one luxuries that such a life afforded.

As the days passed she began to praise the virtues of largesse and before long she was adding her voice to Mrs. Dovedale's in urging Eugenia to be more responsive to the suit of the Marquis. The main strategy of the two older women was to remind her of how indebted she was to the Marquis.

"Why, who do you think paid for the gown you wore on the night of Lady Bescombe's ball?" Great-Aunt Cloris demanded one afternoon. "The ball you did not, after all, attend," she added.

Eugenia blinked fearfully. "Why – *you* did, Great-Aunt Cloris!"

"I most certainly did not!"

Eugenia turned quickly to Mrs. Dovedale. "Mama?"

Her mother shook her head. "It was not me, either, dear. I *did* sell my jewellery in Hatton Garden, but when you were so adamant that you would never forgive me for such an act, I knew I had to get it all back. So I – wrote to the Marquis for help."

"You wrote to the Marquis?" repeated Eugenia faintly.

"Yes, dear. He redeemed the jewellery for me and then insisted on paying for the gowns."

Eugenia remembered the incident at Craven Hill when she had witnessed the Marquis handing her mother a package in the hallway.

Everything – Madame Lefain, the fans, the gloves, the material – everything had been thanks to the intervention of the Marquis!

The revelation made Eugenia miserable. She felt the tentacles of wealth and privilege closing around her.

It was Great-Aunt Cloris who now kept her mother company. Mrs. Dovedale had so far recovered as to be able to get about with a stick and on fine days she and her aunt would sit chatting on the terrace. Eugenia was certain they used these occasions to continue to plot an alliance between herself and the Marquis.

For want of a confidante, Eugenia found herself drawn more and more into the company of Bridget. She knew she was permitting an uncommon degree of intimacy between herself and the maid, but considered this was the price she must pay in order to find any opportunity whatsoever to talk about Gregor.

Bridget continued to puzzle Eugenia. She still seemed sometimes almost driven to stoke Eugenia's interest in Gregor. At other times she would turn sullen and refuse to discuss him at all.

"What could you want with that mad Russian, miss?" she would say. "The Marquis is the catch."

Eugenia would clutch her head in her hands. "Bridget, please! You are sounding just like my mother and my great-aunt."

Bridget, scowling, picked at her cuff. "Well, maybe they're right. *I* wouldn't mind being Mistress of a big place like this."

On these occasions, Eugenia felt that the letter tucked in her bodice was an emblem of the only friend she had in the world. It seemed to throb against her bosom, reminding her of the existence of romantic passion as opposed to calculating common sense.

Though Eugenia cherished the letter from Gregor, she did not dare reply to it. The painter had declared his affections but not his intentions. It was all too incumbent upon Eugenia, as a young unmarried girl, to simply hope and wait for his next move.

No sign had come from Gregor, however, when the next twist in Eugenia's fortunes took place.

Great-Aunt Cloris, after a dish of mussels at lunch, began to feel somewhat queasy and this put her into a bad humour.

"This is what comes of grand living," she grumbled. "It destroys your innards."

"You did consume an unusually large amount," Mrs. Dovedale ventured timidly.

"That is my point!" snapped Great-Aunt Cloris. "Excess is positively encouraged here. I am going to have to go home or I shall surely expire. Oh, I feel quite ill. Bridget, help me from my chair. I must go to my room and lie down."

At about four o'clock, the Marquis appeared to enquire after the health of Great-Aunt Cloris. He had been informed by his butler that the old lady had been taken ill.

Mrs. Dovedale was tremulous in her delight at the Marquis's unexpected visit.

"Oh, oh, how kind of you to ask. She is resting and I am sure will be better by nightfall. You must stay and take some tea with us. You have become quite a stranger, you know."

The Marquis declined. "I understand that Mrs. Dewitt is considering going home," he commented.

Mrs. Dovedale became suddenly flustered. She took the Marquis's remark as a tacit indication that it was time *all* his guests considered going home.

"I am sure she did not mean it. She is very happy here. *I* am very happy here. Indeed – *indeed* – "

Here Mrs. Dovedale took out a large handkerchief and held it to her eyes. "Indeed, I will never in my life be so content as I am at Buckbury. The thought of returning to that cold house in Craven Hill fills me with horror – yes, horror."

"Mama, please do not talk so," Eugenia urged in a low voice.

"I must give vent to my emotions," wailed Mrs. Dovedale. "How is it that fortune is so regularly my foe?"

The Marquis regarded her gravely.

"Believe me, Mrs. Dovedale," he said, "fortune might turn out to be less of a foe than you imagine. Now, please excuse me for such a brief visit. I must attend to other matters."

The first part of the Marquis's words were so cryptic that, as the door closed behind him, Mrs. Dovedale and Eugenia were left quite bewildered.

The following morning, as Eugenia took breakfast in her room, a command came from the Marquis. She was to join him for a ride at ten o'clock.

She resented the peremptory tone of the command. At

the same time, she was intrigued, for it was a tone the Marquis had never used with her before. However she felt, it would undoubtedly contravene good manners to refuse.

So at ten o'clock she presented herself to the Marquis. Two horses were brought to the front of the Abbey. A footman helped her mount and then they were off.

The Marquis seemed grimly bent on making progress rather than simply taking a ride. He led the way down the two miles of gardens towards the river and the woods.

As he guided his horse towards the wooden bridge, Eugenia suddenly felt her heart skip a beat. Surely he was not going to make her revisit the ruins of '*Paragon*'? What cruel trick was this?

"M-my lord," she called but her words were tossed to the air like seedlings, so strong was the breeze.

Deep in the woods, however, the breeze lost its force. Only the treetops swayed and pitched. Down below all was quiet.

"My Lord, I should like to turn back," she pleaded but the Marquis forged on.

At last the trees ended. The Marquis halted and, behind him, Eugenia.

What she saw before her made her gasp. In one instant she understood all.

There stood '*Paragon*' but it was no longer a ruin. The thatch was mended, the walls rebuilt. Glass gleamed in the window embrasures, the shutters and front door were painted a cornflower blue. The cottage had been reborn and it was surely all down to the hand of the Marquis.

Overcome with conflicting emotions, Eugenia burst into tears.

CHAPTER SIX

The Marquis did not dismount. He made no move at all to console Eugenia but waited in respectful silence for her sobs to cease.

All around the clearing, treetops rustled and swayed. A deer started out from the undergrowth, then froze – with eyes as black as mere water, it stood for a moment staring at the two riders before bolting fearfully back into the woods.

Still Eugenia wept. Added to the shock of seeing '*Paragon*' restored to its former modest glory was a sense of deep foreboding. The future was being spun so cunningly about her that she could barely parry its threads.

The Marquis's horse shifted, stepped a few paces back before lowering its head to crop at the grass. The Marquis let the reins trail.

"It seems the restoration of '*Paragon*' does not please Miss Dovedale," he asserted quietly.

Eugenia pressed the back of her hands to her wet cheeks.

"Pardon me, my Lord. It – it does please me. Only I – "

She could not continue. The Marquis regarded her quizzically.

"Only I cannot help but ask myself *why*?" she finished.

The Marquis hesitated before his reply. "I had hoped that was a question you would not ask, Miss Dovedale. I – rather fear the effect of my answer upon your present sensibilities."

"Then by all means, let the subject alone," said Eugenia quickly. She did indeed fear an answer that might amount to a declaration of intent with regard to herself.

Then, realising that her response had been somewhat churlish, she stumbled on. "I would *like* to think that you perhaps undertook the task as a – as a tribute to my father."

The Marquis pondered this. "If it pleases you, Miss Dovedale, you may indeed consider it as a kind of tribute," he said at last.

"It does please me," Eugenia replied simply.

The Marquis nodded gravely, then made a gesture in the direction of the cottage garden. "Now – I wonder if you have noticed the creature grazing by the fence?"

Eugenia turned her head and gave a cry.

"Can it be – is that my pony – Bud?"

"Somewhat stiff of gait, but, yes, it is he."

Eugenia could not believe her eyes. "B-but how did you find him?"

"It was not difficult. When your mother left, she offered him to my housekeeper's nephew. So Bud remained near the estate."

Eugenia slipped from the saddle and ran across to the old pony. She could not be sure that after all this time he would recognise her, but when she threw her arms about his neck, he nuzzled her cheek with great affection. Delighted as she was to see her old friend, part of her was uncomfortably aware that *his* appearance at least could not be explained away as a tribute to her late father.

"I suppose – I suppose my cat is lost?" Eugenia asked without turning her head.

"Alas, yes," came the reply. "He became a famous mouser and died fat and wealthy."

Through what remained of her tears and despite her general misgivings, Eugenia could not help but smile. Encouraged at last, the Marquis invited her to inspect the interior of the cottage.

Giving Bud one last pat, Eugenia followed the Marquis through the front door.

The interior too had been restored. Ceilings and walls were painted ivory, floor boards polished so that they gleamed like honeycomb. Not only that, the rooms were all agreeably furnished.

In the drawing room, curtains hung at the window and a fire was laid in the grate.

"Why, it is ready for occupancy," marvelled Eugenia, her eyes darting into every corner.

"Indeed it is," said the Marquis.

"You have found tenants?" There was a tremor in Eugenia's voice as she asked this question, for now that 'Paragon' looked every inch the home she remembered, she was not sure she relished the idea of strangers living there.

"Yes, I have prospective tenants in mind, if they will accept it," said the Marquis mysteriously.

"If?" Eugenia looked surprised. "Why, who might they be, that they should for one moment consider *not* accepting it? It must be the prettiest cottage on the estate!"

The Marquis regarded her musingly. "I have earmarked the cottage for a mother and daughter whom I know. The mother I am sure will be happy to live here. It is the daughter whose enthusiasm I doubt."

Eugenia gazed at him wonderingly for a moment before she understood.

"You – you mean myself?" she breathed. "And my mother?"

"I do indeed," replied the Marquis.

"But – but we could never afford the rent, my Lord. We live with Great-Aunt Cloris and – help her in the house in return for our lodgings."

"Rent!" frowned the Marquis. "I am not seeking rent. The cottage is yours and your mother's, Miss Dovedale. I had once intended to pass the freehold over to your father. Now I am passing it over to you. The reason for my most recent visit to London was to sign over the freehold. This – is now yours."

With that, the Marquis held out his hand, to reveal in his palm a small yellow key.

Eugenia took the key from him as if it was a gold bar. She held it in trembling fingers, looking from the Marquis to the room around her and back.

"Mine?" she repeated. "*Paragon* is mine?"

"Yours," said the Marquis firmly. "And you may move in this very afternoon, if you so wish."

Eugenia felt giddy at the prospect opening before her. In one fell swoop, to be rendered Mistress of her own home and, by the same token, freed of the obligation to return to Great-Aunt Cloris in London.

Eager to pass on the good news to her mother, Eugenia locked the door of the cottage with the key the Marquis had given her. He went to untie their horses, but Eugenia had other ideas.

"I shall ride Bud home," she declared.

"Let me saddle him up for you," offered the Marquis, intending to use the saddle of the horse that had brought Eugenia to the cottage.

"No, no, I shall ride bareback," she cried gaily. "I always did as a child."

Before the Marquis could reply, Eugenia had grasped Bud's mane and swung herself up on to his white back.

Eugenia broke into an excited gallop for the last half mile of the return, leaving an amused Marquis in her wake.

She burst in upon her mother and Great-Aunt Cloris with such rosy cheeks and sparkling eyes that they were both convinced the Marquis had proposed.

"It is good news, then, Eugenia?" squealed Mrs. Dovedale, hands clasped to her cheeks.

"Yes, Mama!" Eugenia hugged herself with delight. "You will never, never guess what it is."

"I think I might," simpered Mrs. Dovedale. "You are to be – Mistress of Buckbury?"

For an instant only, Eugenia's face clouded. Why must her mother keep harping on the same subject?

"No," she replied shortly. "But I *am* to be Mistress of '*Paragon.*'

Mrs. Dovedale and Great-Aunt Cloris looked at each other in astonishment.

'*Paragon*?' they repeated.

"Yes." Eugenia regarded them triumphantly. "The Marquis has had it restored. It looks just as it used to when we lived there, Mama. The Marquis has signed the freehold over to me. Look. Here is the key."

Hands still to her cheeks, Mrs. Dovedale stared at the key lying in her daughter's palm. The Marquis may not have proposed as expected, but this little yellow key represented a tangible new hope. It was obvious that the Marquis wished to keep Eugenia near him.

Great-Aunt Cloris was not so pleased by this latest turn of events.

"The Marquis might have had the good grace to consult me," she grumbled. "Have I not devoted a good deal of time and money to your upkeep these past few years? And to have the mainstay of my advancing years whisked from under my nose!"

Eugenia ran to her great-aunt and dropped to her knees before her. "Great-Aunt Cloris, you know you are welcome to live with us at '*Paragon*' if you so choose."

"So you have decided to live there?" Great-Aunt Cloris regarded her niece narrowly. "You will not return to London at all?"

Eugenia rocked back on her heels and stared at the floor. "I – think I might return – for a while," she said faintly. "I mean, I will have to – collect some of my belongings."

Her great-aunt had touched on one particular aspect of her good fortune that troubled Eugenia.

Secluded at '*Paragon*', how was she ever going to meet Gregor again?

Mrs. Dovedale misread the frown on her daughter's brow.

"Eugenia, dear, there is really no reason for you to travel to London if you do not wish," she said soothingly. "I can accompany Aunt Cloris home. I can pack your things and bring them back with me. I am sure the Marquis will take you under his wing while I am away."

"Thank you, Mama, but I would not dream of it," she said firmly. "I will return to London myself to collect my own possessions."

Great-Aunt Cloris was brooding. "You two have obviously not considered the full implication of this – new life. You may well own the roof over your head, but how will you pay for its maintenance? How will you pay the butcher and the baker and the candlestick maker?"

"Oh, Aunt Cloris," murmured Mrs. Dovedale dreamily. "Don't you think the Marquis must have plans for my daughter and myself beyond the bestowing of '*Paragon*'?

"You had better hope so," sniffed Great-Aunt Cloris.

This question of how Eugenia and her mother were going to survive without an income at '*Paragon*' was solved the very next day, when the Marquis informed Mrs. Dovedale that he had settled a yearly sum of two hundred and fifty pounds on her in memory of her late husband and his dear friend, Mr. Dovedale.

Mrs. Dovedale brought the news to Eugenia, where she sat writing a list of all she needed from London for her new life at '*Paragon*'.

"We are doubly – triply – indebted to the Marquis now," she said insinuatingly. "We shall have to accede to his every wish."

Eugenia looked up from her notebook. "And if he proposes that we throw ourselves into the fountain, Mama?"

Mrs. Dovedale was shocked. "What a nonsensical thing to say. He would never ask such a thing. I merely meant that – "

Eugenia closed her notebook and stood up. "You merely meant that I should be civil to him, as our benefactor. Well, I shall be very civil. But I shall not encourage him to court me, Mama."

"Stubborn child," her mother muttered under her breath as Eugenia left the room. "Stubborn child."

*

Although Mrs. Dovedale was thrilled to be suddenly in possession of a house and an income, it was some days before she was able to wrench herself away from the luxuries of Buckbury and take up residence in her new abode.

The day came, however, when the trunks belonging to herself, Eugenia, Great-Aunt Cloris and Bridget were sent in an ox-drawn wagon to the cottage.

The four ladies travelled in a carriage, the Marquis following on horseback. He had elected to oversee the unpacking of the wagon himself.

'*Paragon*' was at its most seductive that morning. Smoke curled from the chimneys, curtains fluttered at the open windows, doves cooed from the eaves. Inside, the smell of baking came wafting from the kitchen, where the cook from Buckbury had been set temporarily to work.

Once all the trunks and items of furniture were unpacked and in place, the cook brought tea and scones in to the drawing room.

Mrs. Dovedale beamed at the Marquis. "You think of everything, my Lord! I doubt that there are any other ladies in Rutland treated with such ingenuity."

The Marquis gave a bow, a smile hovering about his lips.

Eugenia felt almost resentful that the Marquis was so assiduous in his attentions, for it made her disinterest seem perverse to the objective eye.

After only a few days at '*Paragon*', it seemed to Eugenia and her mother as if they had never been away. Even Great-Aunt Cloris began to feel at home. It was only Bridget who remained un-reconciled to what she saw as banishment from the comforts of Buckbury.

Although she remained determined to resist his attractions, Eugenia could not but thank the Marquis a thousand times a day in her heart for his generosity. She was happier at '*Paragon*' than she could have believed possible. All that was missing was – Gregor Brodosky.

She still hungered for news of him, details of his person and behaviour such as only Bridget could supply. Eugenia would use the excuse of helping out with the sorting of linen or the preparing of meals, to drink in stories of Gregor and his many exploits. It amazed Eugenia that Bridget was such an unending fount of knowledge. Bridget recounted episode after episode of Gregor's life.

"He killed a wild boar once, on the estate of his uncle."

"A boar!" gasped Eugenia.

"Yes, miss. With his bare hands. He strangled it. He's awfully strong, is Gregor."

Eugenia gave a barely perceptible sigh.

"He was in the Russian Army," continued Bridget, "and – killed a man in a duel. He almost married a Countess, once. She was very rich but – "

Bridget regarded Eugenia slyly from under her dark brows.

"Yes?" Eugenia prompted.

"He didn't love her. He said, '*what's money without love, Bridget*'?"

"Of course." Eugenia gave a solemn nod but her heart was dancing in her breast.

Gregor was just like her. *Just like her!*

The effect of these stories was to create in Eugenia's mind a veritable romantic hero, a man of almost superhuman strength, whose feelings once roused would sweep a girl up as into the wake of whirlwind.

"Will he – be in London – next month?" Eugenia pried shyly. Great-Aunt Cloris had proposed returning home then and Eugenia planned to accompany her.

"Oh, certainly," replied Bridget. "He was all set to paint Lord and Lady Glover's miniatures when we left. He won't have finished those yet."

'*Not long to go*', thought Eugenia, '*before I see my true love again*!'

Meanwhile, Mrs. Dovedale and Great-Aunt Cloris persisted in their campaign to make Eugenia look with a more encouraging eye upon the Marquis. They reminded her time after time of all that he had done for her and how this indicated a deep interest in her happiness and well-being. They never failed, after a visit from the Marquis, to comment upon his good looks, his style, his demeanour and his manners.

"There isn't a lady in the land who would not have him!" sighed Mrs. Dovedale.

"Then let them fight over him, for I shan't!" retorted Eugenia.

She was so sure that her attitude to the Marquis was set in stone that an incident that occurred the following afternoon threw her into some confusion.

The Marquis sent word that he would be bringing a visitor to tea. Mrs. Dovedale set out the china and ordered a fruit loaf to be baked. She, Great-Aunt Cloris and Eugenia waited in the drawing room and at three o'clock precisely the Marquis rode into view.

With him, side-saddle on a black mare, rode a veiled lady.

Mrs. Dovedale looked alarmed. "A lady? Why is he bringing a lady?"

When Bridget announced the Marquis and – a *Lady Walling*, Mrs. Dovedale dropped to the sofa in despair.

"Lady Walling?" she whispered. "That fortune hunter!"

Eugenia regarded the Marquis and his companion closely as they entered. Lady Walling drew up her veil and extended her hand.

"What a charmingly domestic scene this is!" she exclaimed, indicating the merry fire in the hearth and the table set for tea.

Eugenia disliked her instantly. Whether it was this dislike or something else that coloured her subsequent responses she could never decide, but over the course of tea she realised that, much as she was convinced that she herself did not want the Marquis, she was equally convinced that she did not want Lady Walling to have him either!

Lady Walling, lean and bony as she was, nevertheless simpered and pouted at the Marquis as if she was a kitten. The Marquis was all courtesy and attention. Indeed, his eyes barely left Lady Walling's face and Eugenia was surprised to feel herself reddening with indignation. After all, it was Eugenia he usually favoured with his glances.

The Marquis explained to the company the reason for his visit. The hunting season was upon them and he had decided to throw a ball. Lady Walling had agreed to help secure the presence of an orchestra, for there was to be dancing.

"I have thrown many balls at my own place, Walling Hall," boasted Lady Walling, "and I always hire an orchestra. There must be dancing. I myself am a most accomplished dancer."

Eugenia gritted her teeth. "I am sure you are, Lady Walling," she said.

Lady Walling flashed a tight smile. "My legs are long, you see, and very well-formed."

"It is a pity, then," returned Eugenia, "that you are not in a position to wear breeches, the better to reveal them."

Lady Walling might have replied in kind but that the Marquis appeared to have a sudden fit of coughing.

When the Marquis and Lady Walling rose to go, Eugenia noticed for the first time how truly imposing was his physique.

She walked to the window and watched the two of them ride away.

'I do not think *she* is right for him at all,' she told herself sulkily.

All evening, her thoughts flew round and round in her head like birds in a room with closed windows. Images of Gregor fighting a wild boar alternated with images of the Marquis dancing with Lady Walling.

She *knew* that she loved Gregor but it was strange how this did not preclude jealousy – yes, jealousy, she was honest enough to recognise it for what it was – that she had lost dominion over the Marquis. She supposed that her continued defence against his attentions had finally convinced him that he should look elsewhere for romance.

*

Invitations to the ball soon arrived at '*Paragon*'. Despite herself, Eugenia became infected with the atmosphere of excited anticipation. She was unwilling to wear the same gown that she had worn the night of her mother's accident and was relieved when Great-Aunt Cloris agreed to relinquish one of the expensive dresses she had brought with her.

The Marquis sent a gig to collect them.

As Buckbury Abbey came into view amidst the trees the occupants of the gig stared in wonder.

Torches flared brightly all around the house. The windows glowed with candlelight. Footmen with powdered wigs stood sentry on each step that led up to the entrance.

With a thrill, Eugenia remembered that party long ago at Buckbury, when she had tried to reach the star at the top of the Christmas tree.

The ballroom within was a feast of colour and light and laughter. There was the glint of crystal, the whirl of silk and satin, the scent of various exotic perfumes mingling with the tang of orange from the peel laid along the great logs in the marble fireplace.

Mrs. Dovedale and Great-Aunt Cloris wished to scrutinise proceedings from the safety of the velvet benches lining the walls. They assured Eugenia that they were perfectly all right and waved her away.

Eugenia moved among the guests as if in a dream.

She was unaware that she herself looked like a

walking dream, a vision of perfection.

Young men stared at her over the shoulders of their dancing partners. Young ladies frowned and fluttered their fans nervously before their faces.

Her gown was of a deep blue hue and brocaded with gold. Its curved neckline revealed her alabaster shoulders. Her eyes, wide-set and large, gleamed like sapphires in the candlelight.

When the music finished, gentlemen jostled to claim a dance.

As Eugenia began to fill in her card, she could not help but feel a rush of triumph. She wondered if the Marquis was nearby. She did not want him – of course she did not – but she was piqued that he had decided he did not want *her*!

Imagine her chagrin therefore when the Marquis sailed by without a glance in her direction, his arm firmly around the waist of Lady Walling who flashed Eugenia a bright, victorious smile.

Eugenia tossed her head and took up the glass of champagne proffered by a passing footman.

She spluttered as the bubbles tickled her palate. Another sip and her tongue tingled. She finished the glass and took another. Now she began to feel inexplicably carefree.

The music struck up again and she was spun onto the floor for her next dance. At the end of which she accepted another glass of champagne, then another, before she was whirled away in the arms of a young man with large, prune-coloured eyes.

She was enchanted by everything. The music, the attention, the display of wealth, the grandeur of her surroundings. Buckbury was such a beautiful house and – it might have been hers. Quite what she had thrown away was suddenly impressed upon her with renewed force.

The suppers and balls she might have presided over! The gowns she might have acquired!

Eugenia frowned. Lady Walling was *still* dancing with the Marquis.

She twisted her neck left and right to follow the path of the Marquis and his partner. For the first time she noticed how gracefully the Marquis moved. He was a head taller than almost anyone else in the room. His eye was proud and gallant. Why, half the women in the room were watching him. He was quite wasted on Lady Walling!

She suddenly spun away from her astonished partner to seize another glass of champagne. Over the rim, her gaze followed the Marquis's progress.

Mrs. Dovedale appeared at her daughter's elbow.

"Think of all that you owe him, Eugenia," she whispered with great urgency. "Think of how you might repay him. If you do not seize your chance now, all will be lost. He will surely marry Lady Walling."

Eugenia's brow creased as an image of Gregor flashed through her mind. But for once his memory could not compete with the all too potent present. It could not compete with the splendour of the occasion. It could not compete with a sudden, overwhelming sense of moral obligation that dizzyingly coincided with music and magic and twinkling stars.

Forgetting even her self imposed promise never to marry anyone her mother favoured, Eugenia thrust her glass at her mother and stumbled off towards the Marquis and Lady Walling.

Mrs. Dovedale hugged herself in glee.

The dance ended as Eugenia neared the couple. The Marquis caught sight of Eugenia first. One glance seemed to convince him that he must make his excuses to Lady Walling – whose lips formed a perfect 'o' of annoyance in response –

and move quickly to Eugenia's side.

Taking her arm without a word, he steered her towards the French windows that over-looked the terrace. Guests watched them pass and one or two heads bent to whisper conspiratorially.

"I think you may need a little air, Miss Dovedale," the Marquis murmured as he opened a window and guided Eugenia through.

The air made her stagger. She grasped hold of the ironwork that ran along the terrace and gazed misty eyed at the Marquis.

"It is all so – so – so wonderful," she breathed.

"I so am glad that you are – enjoying yourself," said the Marquis, his eyebrow raised.

"Oh, I am! Only – only one thing troubles me, my Lord."

The Marquis cocked his head enquiringly. At the same time his eyes travelled over her face and body with such undisguised hunger that she felt exultant. Why, she might yet have him!

She took a deep breath, and her mind seemed to swim in her head.

"You must not – you *really really* must not – marry Lady Walling."

A wry smile danced at the corners of the Marquis's lips. "Indeed? Then who *may* I marry, Miss Dovedale?"

Eugenia's eyes widened as if she imagined the Marquis a fool to ask.

"Why, me!" she beamed, brightly and innocently. "Me, Eugenia Dovedale."

And with that, she stumbled dazedly into his willing arms.

CHAPTER SEVEN

Eugenia opened her eyes and closed them again quickly. Even through the curtains, the morning light seemed unbearably bright and her head was throbbing like a mill loom. Groaning, she turned her face to the pillow.

The bedroom door creaked and footsteps crossed the floor to the window.

"No – no – " moaned Eugenia. "Don't open the curtains."

"Got to, miss," came Bridget's voice, strangely sullen. "It's past twelve and I was told to wake you. Your mother and great-aunt are all agog to see you. Being as you're now an engaged woman."

Eugenia sat bolt upright in shock. Everything came flooding back to her.

"I – did it," she murmured, her hand to her lips.

"You did it all right, miss." Bridget turned and almost ripped the curtains apart. Light poured in and Eugenia shrouded her eyes. Bridget, hands on hips, regarded her almost balefully.

"You did it, miss," she repeated. "What am I supposed to tell Gregor, eh? I promised I would – I bin doing what he asked – it ain't – isn't – my fault if you lose your head after a few glasses of champagne, is it?"

Tears pricked Eugenia's eyes. "Is that what I did?" she

muttered. "Lost my head? Oh. Oh."

The enormity of what she had done descended on her like a heavy cloud. She sank back upon the pillow.

"You've made your bed," said Bridget with unaccountable bitterness. "Now lie in it."

'*You've made your bed, now lie in it.*'

This phrase became a constant echo in Eugenia's head as the day passed. When the Marquis called in that afternoon, she feigned illness rather than see him before she had absorbed the full extent of what had happened.

She could not believe that after all her fierce resistance she had succumbed to the wishes of the Marquis at a moment when he seemed the least interested in pursuing them.

'It was all the fault of Lady Walling,' she decided. 'If *she* had not set her cap at the Marquis, *I* should not have been similarly tempted.'

This seemed a poor excuse even to Eugenia, but she did not wish to analyse her behaviour in any greater depth. The deed was done. She was engaged. She could not be so dishonourable as to change her mind.

She must banish all thoughts of Gregor. He must now take his place as the great, lost, romantic love of her life. The secret that must lie hidden forever in her heart.

She could not bring herself to admit that she felt a certain strange pleasure in this idea.

Bridget's bitter response to the news was a puzzle. In the end Eugenia decided that the girl was perhaps a little in love with Gregor herself, enough to be jealous on his behalf that the object of his interest, Eugenia, had slipped his noose.

Mrs. Dovedale, of course, was beside herself with delight and Great-Aunt Cloris scarcely less so.

Seated at Eugenia's bedside, both ladies eagerly discussed their plans for the wedding, which would take place at Buckbury early in the New Year.

By the next day, Eugenia had so far marshalled her resources as to be prepared to accept the consequence of her behaviour. Duty and gratitude must be the guiding principle in her relations to the Marquis, she decided. All notions of romantic love must be extinguished from her bosom.

The Marquis called again that afternoon. His eyes lit up as Eugenia entered the room. Eugenia permitted him to kiss her hand and then she glided, eyes lowered, to the sofa.

Mrs Dovedale, who had without compunction allowed Eugenia to ride out unattended with the Marquis when she was single, became convinced that her daughter must be chaperoned at all times now that she was engaged.

Eugenia was grateful for this sudden surge of propriety on her mother's part, for it meant that she and the Marquis were never alone. She did not desire a repetition of the brief intimacy that had occurred the night of the ball.

She retained a fleeting image of his lips bending to hers as she fell into his arms, his hand brushing away a stray curl from her forehead before he escorted her back to the ballroom. She did not care to dwell on the words he had uttered as she had offered up her future to his care – *"my darling, how I have longed for this moment."*

Soon enough she must offer up her body as well as her future. Would she then be able to keep at bay images of Gregor's tousled hair and impassioned presence?

Eugenia was sure that Bridget had informed Gregor of the engagement, but from Gregor himself there came no word, either of admonishment or of passionate regret. Eugenia liked to think that the painter was too heart-broken to respond.

Since Bridget now remained determinedly silent on the subject, all that Eugenia had to remind herself that there had ever been a chance of perfect happiness was the note that he had sent her. She could not bring herself to destroy it as she should, but folded it into a perfume-drenched lace handkerchief which she kept in her reticule.

The Marquis showered his fiancée with gifts. Flowers in great profusion began to adorn her bedroom at '*Paragon*'. Kid gloves, silk scarves and purses began to pile up. Eugenia surveyed all these treasures with a heavy heart. She could see them only as the spoils of her ill-considered conduct rather than what they were – sincere tokens of the Marquis's love.

At last, however, she began to yield to the constant nature of her fiancé's attentions. He did not rush her nor demand more than she felt able to give. He was all courtesy and patience. She began to see her way to being a devoted rather than merely a dutiful spouse.

The sad realisation that she must once again leave the happy confines of '*Paragon*' was tempered by visions of herself as Mistress of one of the great houses of England.

By late November, she was utterly reconciled to her fate. How simply events might then have progressed would never be known, for fate, with the unwitting aid of Great-Aunt Cloris, decided to prove mischievous.

The Marquis was showing his collection of family portraits to Great-Aunt Cloris, Mrs. Dovedale and Eugenia, when Great-Aunt Cloris declared that it was a great pity that there was no portrait of Eugenia in existence.

"She is a beautiful subject, you must admit," she said.

Eugenia blushed under the Marquis's fond gaze.

"Indeed she is," he agreed.

Great-Aunt Cloris gave a sudden clap of her hands.

"That will be my wedding present to you! I shall have a portrait of Eugenia painted to add to your collection."

"Capital!" exclaimed the Marquis.

"I know the very painter," she added with great satisfaction.

Eugenia felt the blood drain from her cheeks. She both knew and dreaded what her great-aunt would say next.

"*Gregor Brodosky*!" she exclaimed. "He painted a handsome portrait of me. Not that I have seen it completed, but there was no question that from the beginning he captured me perfectly – "

Her great-aunt's voice seemed to be coming from far away. Eugenia clutched the back of a chair.

"I don't want – a portrait," she heard herself say faintly.

"Nonsense!" Great-Aunt Cloris waved her hand. "I will have none of this false modesty! It is not up to you, anyway, my girl. It is a matter between myself and the Marquis. It is decided. I shall write and ask Mr. Brodosky to join us here at Buckbury. That is of course – " And here the old lady turned quickly to the Marquis, "that is if my Lord agrees?"

The Marquis hesitated. He was concerned at Eugenia's response and at her sudden pallor.

"Do invite him here," he said. "I should like the portrait to be commenced immediately."

Eugenia felt as if all her hard-won mastery of herself was in danger.

A stone has been cast onto the settled surface of her days. The disturbance spread in vast, unwieldy ripples. She could not control the feelings they stirred up within her breast.

*

Gregor replied to Great-Aunt Cloris's letter that he would be delighted to come to Buckbury. To Eugenia's tremulous surprise – he had after all been silent for quite a while now – he sent, via Bridget, a letter of a more intimate nature entirely.

"*My little treasure, my little nugget of gold, I shall be*

there to stare at you all day and paint and – ha! take advantage of whatever else might be permitted your adoring Gregor."

Bridget watched in amusement as Eugenia read the letter.

"Well, miss?"

"He writes that – he will be glad to see me again." said Eugenia.

"So he will be, miss. And you'll be glad to see him. You'll find out that you've made a mistake!"

"You – you are a fool," retorted Eugenia, becoming angry with herself for having read the letter at all. She should have torn it up before Bridget's very eyes. "How can marrying the Marquis – who loves me and offers me a secure future – be a mistake?"

Bridget shrugged. "It is if you dream of someone else kissing you, miss."

"Oh, do go away, Bridget. I care not a jot for Gregor Brodosky. I am happy to be engaged to the Marquis."

Bridget closed the door behind her with a smirk. Eugenia waited for a moment to be sure that the maid would not return, then she folded Gregor's letter and tucked it into her reticule.

Now she harboured two guilty secrets from the eyes of the Marquis.

She really must destroy these letters before the wedding.

At the thought of the wedding her brow clouded. She rose and paced the floor.

Perhaps there was a hidden meaning to all this. Perhaps her commitment to the Marquis must be tested as in a fire for its strength and durability. Yes, that was it!

This idea almost soothed her, for it enabled her to set

herself a task. To muster all her powers of self-restraint to overcome this resurgence of romantic interest in Gregor.

She began to almost relish the challenge.

Yet on the day of Gregor's arrival, as she waited with the Marquis, Mrs. Dovedale and Great-Aunt Cloris in the hall at Buckbury to greet the painter, her heart faltered. She could not be still, but moved from window to window, sinking into one chair and then springing up again to sit in another.

Bridget – hair plaited for the occasion and rosewater sprinkled over her bosom – watched Eugenia slyly from under her brows.

"Do sit down, Eugenia, you are making me nervous!" demanded Mrs. Dovedale.

"She seems somewhat feverish," remarked Great-Aunt Cloris. "I hope she has not caught a cold."

The Marquis turned to observe his fiancée. She caught his eye, flinched under his gaze and looked away.

"There is nothing wrong with me," she said. "I am restless, that is all. It's the – the wind in the chimney. It has that effect on me."

"Perhaps I should send for a shawl," began Mrs. Dovedale.

"No, Mama, no, I don't want one. Oh, listen, listen! A carriage is drawing up outside."

All present turned to the door. The Marquis signalled. A footman opened the door and went out. A horse neighed, someone issued instructions. The word 'boxes' was heard. A second later Gregor Brodosky bounded into the hall.

Eugenia felt faint.

He looked as wild and as intemperate as ever. His startling green eyes swept over the assembled company and came to light on Eugenia. Loosening his green velvet cape, he strode over to her and grasped her hand, seemingly unconcerned with the normal proprieties of greeting one's host first.

"My delicious subject," he said mockingly, raising her hand to his lips. "How I have missed you."

She tried to speak, but could not. Her lips parted but no sound issued forth. The hand that Gregor held began to tremble violently.

Her eyes met those of the Marquis.

His stare was black and troubled. Jaw clenched, he regarded her, and her heart sank at sight of the dark shadow crossing his stern, unyielding brow.

*

The following weeks seemed to Eugenia to be the most difficult of her life.

Every day she sat for Gregor. A chair, draped in red velvet, was set up on a dais in the library.

The role of chaperone to Eugenia was performed by Great-Aunt Cloris, Mrs. Dovedale and Bridget in rotation, depending on their other duties.

Posed three-quarters on to Gregor, Eugenia could not see him at work, but was intensely aware of his heated scrutiny. At times she felt herself blushing, certain that his gaze at that moment was lingering on some delicate portion of her anatomy.

When either of the two elder ladies were present, Gregor was all courtesy and circumspection.

When it was Bridget who accompanied Eugenia to a sitting, however, it was a different matter entirely.

Gregor found a thousand reasons to rearrange Eugenia's skirt, draw her gown a little lower on the shoulder, loosen her hair so that it spread out like a mantle. Eugenia could not find it in herself to protest. For one thing she was unsure of what was normally permitted a figure so authoritative as a painter.

For another she experienced a forbidden pleasure at his touch.

He was altogether mercurial. One morning he placed a spray of freshly plucked mistletoe on her lap. Another he ignored her entirely. Sometimes he sang as he painted, songs in Russian, that by their yearning tone Eugenia decided were love songs. Sometimes he addressed Bridget as if Eugenia was not present.

"Why should she wish to marry this Marquis? What does an Englishman know of great desire, of passion?" And he would strike his chest and sigh. "Only a Russian can love a woman as she should be loved."

"P-please, I beg you," whispered Eugenia. "It is wrong to speak like that. Just as it was wrong to send me that last letter when you knew I was engaged. Please. Do not – torment me in this manner."

"Torment you? I?" Gregor turned an ingenuously puzzled gaze upon her. "You think this is torment? If you would yield to me, dear angel, dear treasure, you would know what true torment was. The torment of the flesh, of warm lips, heart beating against heart. Would she not, Bridget?"

Bridget, eyes wide and absorbed, nodded as she chewed the end of her plait.

"Shall we show her, Bridget?" continued Gregor mischievously. Again Bridget nodded and then gasped as Gregor swept her into his arms and kissed her violently on the lips.

Eugenia closed her eyes as a lightening fork of jealousy seared through her. Was there something more intimate between Gregor and Bridget than she had imagined? After all, they had had plenty of time alone together in the kitchen of the house at Craven Hill –

She struggled with her conscience, but Gregor acted upon her sensibilities like a magnet, rendering her powerless to banish him. She was under his spell.

'*Once the painting is finished – once I am married – will be time enough to be without him,*' she told herself.

She might have found strength of purpose in the person of her fiancé, but the Marquis began to change in his behaviour towards her and indeed towards the household in general. He was sharp in tone and withdrawn in manner. With Eugenia he was as courteous as ever, but it was a courtesy that was increasingly as cold as frost. Even Mrs. Dovedale and Great-Aunt Cloris noticed.

"The Marquis seems to be out of sorts entirely," remarked Mrs. Dovedale with a worried frown.

"No doubt it is nerves, Florence, nerves," said Great-Aunt Cloris, with no great conviction. "All gentlemen are so as their marriage approaches."

"Why should he have so greatly altered in his attitude towards you, my daughter?" Mrs. Dovedale continued.

Eugenia looked up quickly. "Is it really so, Mama?"

"Come, come, you cannot be unaware. When did he last request a walk with you or accompany you on a ride about the estate?"

"The latter is not possible, since neither you nor my great-aunt nor Bridget, my chaperones, are able to ride," Eugenia reminded her mother.

Mrs. Dovedale looked exasperated. "Eugenia, you know what I mean! He hardly seeks your company at all these days. If we dine together he hardly looks your way. It is a mercy that he troubles to come to the library when you are sitting. And then he stands like a sentry, all stiff and wordless."

"He would hardly dare interrupt the work of a great artist like Gregor," interceded Great-Aunt Cloris.

"Great artist, indeed!" muttered Mrs. Dovedale. "Who says that fellow is a great artist?"

"Oh, but he is," cried Eugenia. "He pours his whole soul into his painting."

Mrs. Dovedale regarded her daughter narrowly. "Is that all he pours his whole soul into, daughter?"

Eugenia coloured. "Of course."

"Only I am beginning to wonder if there is some connection between the Marquis's seeming – withdrawal of attentions and – this Gregor Brodosky or whatever he is called."

"Impossible!" Eugenia declared. "Gregor is – is quite taken with – with Bridget. Why, I even saw him kiss her – !"

To Eugenia's relief, this last piece of information seemed to satisfy her mother and she took up other, less contentious subjects, with Great-Aunt Cloris.

Eugenia remained brooding over her embroidery.

It was true that the Marquis often appeared unannounced in the library when Gregor was at work.

Eugenia felt guilty that she did not welcome her fiancé's presence. His brooding gaze disconcerted her. It was as if he saw deep into her fickle heart.

One day Gregor was re-arranging Eugenia's foot, where it rested on a footstool, when she looked over his bowed head to see the Marquis watching the scene from the doorway.

"M-my Lord," she stammered.

"My Lady," he replied somewhat sardonically.

Gregor rose and turned to face the Marquis.

"This is an exquisite ankle Eugen – Miss Dovedale has," he remarked, running his paint stained fingers through his unruly hair. "Do you not think so – *my Lord*?"

"Sight of a young lady's ankle is not generally permitted to a mere fiancé, Mr. Brodosky," replied the Marquis coolly.

"Ah." Gregor shrugged. "A pleasure to come."

The Marquis stepped forward. "By gad, you overstep the mark, man!" he growled in a low voice.

Gregor raised his hands in mock apology. "What do I know of – these bourgeois conventions – what you *can* say – what you *cannot* say? I am a free spirit."

The Marquis's jaw clenched. "Make sure you are not *too* free!" he snarled, before turning on his heels and departing.

Bridget gave a little giggle which she quickly suppressed when she saw Eugenia's horror-struck countenance.

"Oh, Eugenia, my flower, do not fret," murmured Gregor soothingly. "Let us all run away together, you and me and Bridget."

Eugenia blinked away incipient tears. "*B – Bridget*?"

Gregor tossed back a lock of dark hair. "Why not? How can I bear to deprive you of a maid?"

Eugenia glanced at Bridget but she was now twirling her plait around her finger while staring at the floor.

"I could not do such a thing – to the Marquis," Eugenia said with a catch in her throat.

Gregor shrugged. "Perhaps the Marquis would not be as unhappy as you think," he said, before taking up his brush again.

*

This exchange with Gregor haunted Eugenia all afternoon and evening. In her bed that night she lay turning his words over and over in her mind.

'*Let us run away together. Perhaps the Marquis would*

not be as unhappy as you think. Let us all run away together.
Perhaps the Marquis would not be so unhappy – '

Could it indeed be possible, she wondered, that the Marquis himself now had serious reservations about their marriage? Could it be that he was beginning to regret his decision?

The longer she considered this, the stronger became her conviction that the Marquis would indeed welcome an escape from the situation in which he now found himself. Then – and Eugenia hardly dared ponder this most seductive of scenarios – then indeed Gregor might take her away and make her his very own.

She resolved to approach the Marquis and offer him his freedom the very next evening.

Eugenia turned to her mother. "If you will excuse me, mother, I wish to go and speak to my – fiancé."

She spoke the word 'fiancé' with the conviction that it might be the last time it was uttered as a mark of her relationship to the Marquis.

"Alone," she added.

Mrs. Dovedale hesitated. "Alone?"

"Yes. It must be so."

"Very well. No doubt the Marquis will send you home in his carriage."

Eugenia watched her mother depart and then hurried to the Marquis's study.

The door was ajar. She pushed it further open and then hesitated.

The Marquis sat at his desk, facing the door. Though he held a pen in his hand he was not writing, but was staring into space. With a start, his eye settled on Eugenia.

It was some time since the two had been alone together and he seemed taken aback. He put down the pen and rose.

"To what do I owe this – this honour, Miss Dovedale?" he asked coldly.

Eugenia closed the door behind her and advanced. The Marquis observed her with a strange curl to his lip. At last she stood trembling before the desk.

"I have come – to offer you – your freedom," she started falteringly.

The Marquis seemed for a moment not to understand.

"I believe you have – ceased to be happy with the idea of – marrying me," she continued. "And I felt that it would be better for us to withdraw from a union that – seems no longer to promise a felicitous life together."

The Marquis's response was not what she had expected. He sprang from behind the desk and grasped her face in his hands, tilting her head so that his eyes might bore into hers. His eyes glittered dangerously.

"You thought yourself in a position to decide my future for me, did you?" he thundered. "Who has put you up to this – this perfidious behaviour?"

"N-no one, my Lord!"

His eyes searched her face in a manner that was both hungry and enraged at one and the same time.

"I do indeed wish to change my plans as regards our marriage, Miss Dovedale," he said through gritted teeth.

"Be assured – I will accept your decision without protest, my Lord," murmured Eugenia, flinching under his painful touch.

"Good. Then I am pleased to inform you that I wish our marriage to go ahead as planned, except in one respect and one respect only. I wish to bring the date of its execution forward."

Eugenia shuddered. Had he deliberately chosen the word 'execution' to alarm her? That was suddenly how she herself viewed the event – an execution, not a celebration.

Suddenly she wished with all her might not to be allied to this man, displaying now a cruel forcefulness of manner at which she had never previously guessed.

"B-but is that w-wise, my lord? The invitations are already sent out. And m-my mother is making my dress herself and has only time enough to finish it as it is. And m-my portrait is nowhere near finished."

This last reason was a mistake, for it seemed to inflame the Marquis still further.

"Do you forget your position, madam?" he roared. "You are beholden to me for everything now. Most of all for '*Paragon*.' Where would you and your mother go if I turned you out? Back to the charity of your great-aunt?"

With a strength she never suspected she possessed, Eugenia pummelled at the Marquis's breast until with an oath he threw her violently aside, so violently she nearly fell. Steadying herself on the edge of the desk, she summoned the breath necessary to reply.

"You – cannot evict us from '*Paragon*'. It is – mine now. You gave me the key."

"So I did, madam. But I did not give you this." Pulling open a drawer in the desk, the Marquis threw a document on the table.

"W-what is that?"

"The deeds. The deeds that prove your ownership."

Without thinking, Eugenia reached for the document, but to her dismay the Marquis snatched it up and began to shred it before her very eyes.

Faced with this uncharacteristic act of cruelty, Eugenia began to back out of the room.

"You are a *brute*, sir. I would not have guessed it. A brute."

The Marquis grew pale at her words. With a groan he plunged his head into his hands.

"If I am, madam, it is your doing," he murmured in despair.

Eugenia did not hear these last words, for she had turned and fled from the room.

Not wishing to ask for the carriage, she was forced to return on foot to '*Paragon*'. She half-ran, half stumbled, her skirt soon hemmed in mud, her slippers soaked.

All the while her thoughts were racing. She would not give in to the Marquis, she would not! His behaviour was outrageous. Passionate, certainly, as she might once have wished, but – outrageous. She would not remain a moment longer on the estate, even if it meant quitting her beloved '*Paragon*'.

She burst through the door of the cottage determined to inform her mother that they were leaving. But when, through the open door of the parlour, she caught sight of her mother seated happily before the fire, she wavered. The flames in the grate leapt high, devouring a mound of logs such as would never have been provided under Great-Aunt Cloris's parsimonious regime at Craven Hill.

Looking slowly around the room, Eugenia realised the extent to which her mother had made herself at home. This was a warm and cosy kingdom over which Mrs. Dovedale might comfortably reign. How could Eugenia take this away from her?

She felt as though her heart was a kite tugged hither and thither in the wind.

Gregor or the Marquis? One final look at her mother gave her the answer.

With a sigh she trailed up to her room. She sat down at her desk and began to write. It was a letter to the Marquis and in it she humbly agreed to his wish to bring the date of their wedding forward.

CHAPTER EIGHT

Eugenia leaned her hand on her chin and gazed out from the carriage that was bearing herself and the Marquis to the lakeside hotel where they were to spend their honeymoon.

They had been married that very morning. Mrs. Dovedale had been puzzled that the date had been brought forward, but secretly relieved. She had begun to fear, considering the Marquis's change of attitude towards Eugenia, that the marriage might never take place at all.

Eugenia found no opportunity to discover *directly* what Gregor thought of the change of plans. The Marquis had quietly indicated to Mrs. Dovedale that he no longer felt it appropriate for Bridget to act as chaperone during the sittings. Mrs. Dovedale, paling at the implication, quickly agreed that from then only she herself or Great-Aunt Cloris would maintain the role.

Gregor, prevented by these two stern guardians from approaching Eugenia, made his displeasure felt by ignoring her completely. He painted on in sullen, frenetic silence. Eugenia was miserable but resigned.

Indirectly, of course, Gregor used Bridget to convey to Eugenia the full extent of his disappointment. The maid handed Eugenia a piece of paper folded into two.

'*My heart breaks as only a Russian heart breaks. Run*

away with me before it is too late. How can you set money against the thrill of passion in the blood?'

This letter, too, joined his two previous letters in Eugenia's reticule. She promised herself that she would dispose of all three – soon!

She dared not reply by pen, but she tremblingly asked Bridget to explain to Gregor that she felt it incumbent upon her to carry out her duty rather than to pursue her desires.

"He won't think much of that, miss," said Bridget with a hint of contempt. "He don't hold with all those notions of *duty*."

"No," sighed Eugenia. "I suppose he doesn't."

She longed for some words of consolation from Bridget, but the maid still stood at the pier glass, as if mesmerised by what she saw there.

"Gregor said he might paint me next," she murmured, head on one side. "Do you think I'd be a good – subject – my Lady?"

The wedding had taken place in the Chapel at Buckbury Abbey. Mrs. Dovedale and Great-Aunt Cloris drove in the gig. Eugenia had requested that if the day was fine she be allowed to ride side-saddle on Bud to the venue.

After their heated encounter at Buckbury and Eugenia's subsequent capitulation, the Marquis had taken himself off to London. He seemed to have no further appetite for the wedding preparations. He did not return from London until two days before the event and was accompanied by Lord and Lady Granton. Lord Granton had agreed to give Eugenia away.

In his absence Eugenia had plenty of time to mull over her fiancé's uncharacteristic behaviour. She wondered guiltily how much her own emotional vacillation – obviously more evident to her fiancé than she had realised – had contributed to the intensity of his outburst. There were times when the memory of the encounter made her shiver. *What manner of man was she was about to wed?*

She turned her head now and threw a glance at the Marquis where he sat in the carriage. He was opposite, leaning his head back against the upholstery, fingers folded over his silver-topped cane. She could not decipher his expression – nor had she been able to do so that morning when she had ridden up to the steps of the Chapel where he and Lord Granton waited.

It had been a frosty morning. Hoar lay over every bough and every blade. The whole day seemed to glisten under a merciless white winter sun.

Her ivory dress lay in a sheath about her, like the petals of a white rose. A white ermine stole covered her shoulders. Silver clasps fastened her golden hair and these glinted as she approached. A silver band held her half veil in place.

The Marquis caught his breath at the sight of her, but his stern expression did not flicker. His eyes smouldered broodingly as she ascended the Chapel steps on the arm of Lord Granton.

Only at the moment when the officiating parson pronounced them man and wife and the Marquis lifted the veil to kiss her lips, did his pupils, meltingly dark, indicate his satisfaction at the binding of Eugenia to him.

Now they were on their way to the place where she would yield her entire person.

She marvelled at how calm she felt.

'*Will I still feel like me tomorrow?*' she asked herself. She turned back and regarded her reflection in the carriage window. Her eyes stared back, wide and wondering.

Eugenia settled back in her seat. Again she watched the landscape roll by beyond the window. Dusk was falling and the hills were mere silhouettes against the darkening sky.

They had been travelling for hours, away from

Buckbury, away from her mother and great-aunt and Lord and Lady Granton. Away from Gregor. She felt a wave of loneliness and homesickness engulf her, even though she knew that soon few of these people would themselves remain on the estate.

By tomorrow, Lord and Lady Granton would be on their way back to London. Mrs. Dovedale and Great-Aunt Cloris would travel with them, but within a month they would be en route to Italy to undertake a tour of that country, a tour proposed and paid for by the Marquis.

They would be accompanied by a new lady's maid, one who had worked for Lady Granton, because Eugenia had insisted that Bridget act as *her* lady's maid during the honeymoon.

She had not informed the Marquis until his return from London. He was understandably reluctant to agree to the presence of Bridget on his honeymoon, but Eugenia was so adamant, citing her need for a familiar face on this, her first trip away from her mother, that at last he gave his grudging approval.

Eugenia could not of course divulge her real reason for wishing Bridget to come away with her, rather than continue to attend Great-Aunt Cloris. The truth was she could not bear to think of Bridget in London and at Craven Hill, which establishment Gregor was bound to visit during the period that Great-Aunt Cloris and Mrs. Dovedale were present before their trip abroad.

There was no doubt that Bridget had guessed at the reason for her new appointment. Although she relished the cachet of being maid to the wife of a Marquis, she was resentful that she was not trusted to remain where she would have access to Gregor and he to her. Eugenia had no doubt that the maid would now feel herself free to throw her own cap at the painter.

Gregor would be the last of the company to leave Buckbury. He had claimed he needed an extra week to work on the portrait of Eugenia, which he had not been able to complete in time for the wedding once the date had been brought forward. The Marquis agreed to Gregor's request to stay on, but added that he wanted to see neither hide nor hair of him by the time he and Eugenia returned from honeymoon.

Gregor had given a mocking bow and promised to have departed well before then.

'My lost love,' thought Eugenia with a catch in her throat before shaking herself.

'*You are married. You must stop this dream of a different kind of love.*'

Beyond the window a moon was rising out of a great expanse of dim water. Lake Caldermere. They must be near the hotel!

Soon the carriage was swinging in through great iron gates and bowling along a dark, elm-lined drive. Eugenia's heart began to beat faster. She placed her hand on her breast, breathing deeply.

"My Lady?" asked the Marquis anxiously.

She shook her head. "I am – all right, my Lord."

When the carriage came to a halt and the steps were lowered, the Marquis handed her down with great solicitude.

The hotel was luxurious but discreet. Their luggage was carried along thick carpets to their suite on the first floor. Bridget was escorted to the room assigned to her along the corridor and the Marquis and Eugenia stood alone in their own chamber.

Eugenia's eyes settled on the richly canopied bed that was the main feature. She felt faint as she imagined what must soon take place.

The Marquis noticed and drew her gently to him.

"There is nothing to fear," he said, with a tenderness in his voice that she had not heard for some time. "I – could never hurt you in any way, my dearest."

"Y-you did before," Eugenia reminded him, lowering her gaze.

"Ah." The Marquis was silent for a moment. "It galls me to think of it. But I was driven by a terrible fear."

"Fear, my Lord?"

"That this present joy might never be mine! But come. You are tired and surely hungry. I am not such a – *brute* – as to put my pleasure before your well-being! I shall leave you while you change for supper."

Eugenia was grateful for the faint twinkle that she detected in the Marquis's eye as he bowed low and departed.

Once alone, however, she sank into despondency. It was with a great effort that she rang for Bridget to help her dress for supper.

Despite the fact that she had not been able to eat breakfast or indeed take any refreshment during the long journey, Eugenia found herself at table merely toying with the salmon laid before her. It was only at the Marquis's urging that she finally forced herself to swallow a few mouthfuls, if only to placate him.

He gently teased her, wondering aloud whether this was the same girl who had flown eagerly from dish to dish when he had first met her at Lady Granton's soirée, and she marvelled at the way in which he had begun to revert to his old self.

She sensed his secret hope – that at last having her all to himself, removed from the seductive presence of Gregor, he might encounter no further obstacle to winning her full affections.

It made her uncomfortable to dwell on this thought and so she began to ask him about his former life. Eventually she touched on the question of the Countess whom, all those years ago, he had followed to France.

The Marquis, interpreting her apparent interest as the usual wifely desire to discover the secrets of her husband's romantic past, smiled at her. He twirled his wine glass in his hand as he replied,

"My reasons for travelling to France – and then remaining there – I have explained. I did not wish my wards to be torn from their native land after being so cruelly orphaned. But, yes, I was drawn to the Countess, though on closer acquaintance I found her to be – not the woman I had hoped."

"Oh." Eugenia's hand strayed to her napkin, the corner of which she began to fold and refold nervously.

"Eugenia," explained the Marquis gently, "a man of my experience has – in the common way of things – become connected with many women who appealed to me in one way or another.

"But my heart never found a home until I laid eyes on you again in London. Perhaps I had always been secretly in love with the little girl who twirled for me in her new dress at the Buckbury Christmas party, all those years ago!"

Eugenia scrunched the napkin tight in her fist. She wanted to respond in kind, to offer up a similar hint of affectionate memory, but she felt paralysed. At last she threw down the napkin and pushed her plate away.

"I – I cannot eat any more – my Lord."

The Marquis dropped his eyes and was silent for a moment. Then he pulled back his chair. "It has been a long day," he said. "Let us retire to our rooms."

Seated a little later before the dressing table while Bridget brushed her hair, Eugenia stared at herself in the mirror. The Marquis had gone to his dressing room, leaving her alone with her maid to prepare herself for the night ahead. Her huge eyes glimmered in the candlelight with unshed tears.

"Don't you cry, miss," said Bridget hotly. "You plumped for this, so you did. You've upset a lot of plans, so you have."

Eugenia tasted salt as the tear reached her lip. "What do you mean by 'plans', Bridget?"

Bridget opened her mouth to reply and then checked herself. "Nuthin," she muttered. "Only – I'm sorry you ain't going to know what real passion is!"

"Do *you* know, Bridget?" asked Eugenia mournfully.

Bridget leaned in close. "It's like nothing else at all. Your flesh is all fever and you want to die, so you do."

The maid straightened quickly as the Marquis entered. Eugenia, quickly wiping the tear from her lip, made a tremulous nod of dismissal and Bridget hurried away.

The Marquis advanced. Eugenia could see his reflection in the mirror and could see the way he hungrily devoured her image, taking in the curve of her breasts beneath her silk negligee and the milky white pallor of her flesh in the flickering candlelight. Her red lips parted in painful anticipation. She felt a wave of guilt that she could not return his ardour in kind.

The Marquis caught up a handful of her golden hair and raised it to his lips. Eugenia stiffened as he then leaned forward and delicately, tenderly kissed the exposed nape of her neck.

With that, Eugenia – tired, exhausted and terrified of the unending conflict within her bosom – plunged her face in her hands and burst into tears.

She felt the Marquis pull away. After a moment she raised her tear-stained face to the mirror. The Marquis stood like someone struck through the heart. The sadness in his eyes was unmistakable.

Eugenia tried to curb her sobs.

"M-my Lord – !"

The Marquis raised a weary hand. "Say nothing, madam. All is only too clear."

"But my Lord – "

With a bitter smile, the Marquis moved away. "Good-night, madam."

Eugenia stared after him wonderingly. "You – you are leaving me here, sir?"

The Marquis paused at the door. "Madam," he said softly, "I will never take to my bed a woman whose heart so obviously lies elsewhere."

With that, he was gone. Eugenia stared after him, hand to her heaving breast, alone to muse upon the consequences of her too divided heart.

*

She was a wife yet not a wife. *A wife in name only*. How she lamented this unnatural state of suspension. Morning after morning she rumpled the bedclothes to look as if both she and the Marquis had slept there. She could not bear for Bridget to know the truth, which was that the Marquis spent every night on the sofa in his dressing room.

During the day he proved as polite and attentive to Eugenia as she supposed it was possible for him to be in the circumstances. They sometimes took walks together around the lake or drove to see some ruin or great house in the area. That these excursions were undertaken in near total silence was a fact unsuspected by Bridget or the Marquis's valet or anyone else at the hotel.

Most of the time the Marquis left her very much to herself. He went hunting with the proprietor of the hotel or fished on the lake.

Eugenia tried to pretend to Bridget that she welcomed

these periods of solitude. Alone in her room, she attempted to read or embroider.

At supper she and the Marquis exchanged pleasantries and nothing more. The Marquis's forbidding brow rendered her too timid to broach the subject of their conjugal relations.

The inevitable result of the prolonged tension, the sleepless nights and the lack of nourishment – for her appetite had still not improved – was that one morning Eugenia felt too dispirited to rise. When Bridget entered with a basket of freshly laundered linen she discovered her Mistress still lying curled on her side under the counterpane, her breakfast tray untouched.

Bridget set the basket down. "What's the matter, my Lady?"

Eugenia's reply was barely perceptible. "I feel – unwell."

Bridget leaned over and felt Eugenia's forehead. "You're hot, all right. Wonder what it is?" Somewhat insensitively, she gave a throaty chuckle. "It's too early for symptoms of – *that*, my Lady! Or is it?"

Fully understanding Bridget's insinuation, Eugenia became flustered.

"No, no, it is not possible – not in a thousand years – for the Marquis will not – has not – slept in this bed. Not for one single night!"

Her voice trailed away and, fist to her mouth, she pressed her cheek into the pillow.

Bridget's eyes were wide. She gave a long, low whistle.

"That's how it stands, eh? Well I never." She stared at Eugenia for a moment and then seemed to suddenly make up her mind as to how she would proceed. She sat on the edge of the bed and stroked Eugenia's damp brow.

"There, there," she said soothingly. "It'll all work out for the best. You'll see."

Eugenia, exhausted, closed her eyes. Bridget continued to stroke her brow until Eugenia's breathing steadied. Then the maid rose carefully and tiptoed from the room.

Around noon, Eugenia woke with a start. She remembered that she had unburdened herself and felt a sense of utter relief that she was no longer all alone with the unpalatable truth, even if her confidante was only Bridget. She must, however, extract a promise from Bridget that she would discuss the matter with no one but herself. She did not want her mother or great-aunt finding out.

With this in mind, she sat up and rang the bell that connected with Bridget's room. When Bridget had not appeared after ten minutes she rang again.

A few minutes later the hotel maid popped her head round the door. "Were you ringing for Bridget, my Lady? Only she's gone off to the village to post a letter. She didn't want to wait until the hotel collection."

Eugenia wrinkled her brow for a moment. To whom was Bridget writing from the hotel?

"Can I help you with anything, my Lady?" asked the hotel maid.

"Thank you, yes. I should like to dress."

Eugenia was still puzzling over Bridget's unaccustomed letter writing as she entered the dining room for lunch, but when the Marquis turned to watch her approach the resolute expression on his face proved a distraction.

"I have made a decision, madam," he announced as the waiter drew out her chair.

The Marquis waited until the waiter had moved away before continuing,

"Since neither of us is deriving the benefit we might from our sojourn here at the lake, I propose that we return to Buckbury tomorrow."

"And – and then?" ventured Eugenia.

The Marquis took up his napkin and shook it out. "And then, madam, we shall, for the foreseeable future, continue this charade. I shall, of course, encourage you to spend as much time as you wish at "*Paragon*", once your mother returns from her trip abroad."

The Marquis regarded her coldly. "Did you imagine that I was about to set you free – Eugenia? Is that what you want?"

The sound of her name on his lips made her start. "I – I don't know what I want, my Lord. I wish I did. And I don't know what – what *you* want."

"I want," replied the Marquis icily, "what is mine. Whatever form such possession takes."

Eugenia did not know what further to say. She did not know if she was relieved or distressed to hear that the present impasse between herself and her husband would continue unchanged.

Bridget's eyes gleamed when she learned that they were to return early to Buckbury. She hummed as she set about packing.

"*You* are happy, at least," commented Eugenia.

"Oh, I am, miss. I don't like it here. I like it at '*Paragon*'.

Eugenia was surprised that Bridget had said '*Paragon*' and not London, where Gregor must by now be residing. Perhaps Bridget had found a beau amongst the young men who worked on the Buckbury estate. That might explain the letter she had sent yesterday, though Eugenia wondered which of the estate workers would actually be able to read.

It was also strange that Bridget had said '*Paragon*' when from now on it was Buckbury that was to be her home, Unless – unless the maid half suspected that the Marquis meant to relegate his wife to her mother's company as much as possible in future!

They returned to Buckbury the following day and life fell into much the same pattern as at the hotel. The Marquis was perfectly civil to his wife before the servants, but in private he was distant, performing the barest of courtesies.

After supper he escorted Eugenia to what had been designated the 'bridal chamber' and bade her goodnight at the threshold, making his way alone to the room he had slept in before his marriage.

During the day Bridget was little company. She performed her chores willingly but otherwise made herself absent at every opportunity. Eugenia assumed she was meeting the lover she had written to from the lakeside hotel. She did not question Bridget nor chide her for not being at her Mistress's beck and call. Eugenia genuinely wished her maid happier than herself in the matter of romance.

Of the portrait of Eugenia painted by Gregor there was no mention. She saw it, shrouded in a sheet, propped up in the Marquis's study. She did not dare ask to look at it and the Marquis never offered.

It was not long before she began to despair of ever leading anything approaching a 'normal' life again. She did not even have the diversion of a busy social round, for the Marquis did not care to accept invitations to dine with his neighbours.

He was, however, at home to callers and one of the most persistent was Lady Walling. Soon Lady Walling was appearing every day for tea.

Eugenia was expected to preside as hostess on these occasions. She poured the tea, proffered the sandwiches, smiled weakly and listened politely to Lady Walling's constant chatter.

Try as she might, her dislike of Lady Walling intensified with each visit. She soon began to suspect that Lady Walling knew that all was not well with the Marquis's marriage.

"There are rumours that your bride does not exist, my Lord," Lady Walling said one afternoon, blinking sweetly over the rim of her cup. "You do rather hide her away here. Anyone would think you were ashamed of her!"

"Anyone can think what they please," replied the Marquis with a shrug. "We – do not care for Society, my wife and I."

Lady Walling placed her free hand on her breast. "Then I am truly honoured that you should care to admit *me* to your circle, my Lord. I am glad of it for I have come to depend upon your hospitality when I ride out each day."

Eugenia could remain silent no longer. "Yes, you seem to consider us a veritable tea-shop, Lady Walling."

The Marquis sat suddenly very still in his chair, while Lady Walling perceptibly bristled.

"I may not be *your* ideal customer, my Lady," she spluttered, "but I do appear to be sincerely welcomed in other quarters."

Eugenia reddened. Lady Walling could mean, of course, that she was welcomed *generally* at houses in the neighbourhood. Or she could mean exactly what Eugenia took her to mean – that she was welcomed *particularly* at Buckbury, by the Marquis if not by his wife.

Her suspicions about Lady Walling were daily compounded by Bridget, who never failed to take the opportunity to allude to the frequency of her visits.

On this particular afternoon, when Eugenia returned to her chamber with such a heated expression, Bridget regarded her Mistress with the eye of someone wondering if a chicken was fattened enough for the feast.

"Are you all right, my Lady?" she asked carefully.

"No. No, I am not! This place is becoming like a prison to me! How I wish I could get away!"

Bridget took a deep breath. "Why don't you and I take a ride to '*Paragon*', my Lady?" she suggested soothingly. "You always find it peaceful there."

'*Paragon*?' Eugenia repeated listlessly. "Yes. Why not? It has indeed always been a haven."

"Of course it's been a haven, my Lady. You freshen yourself up while I get some things together that we might need – "

Eugenia lifted her head. "Things?"

"Some – some refreshment, in case we get hungry. A lantern, in case we stay late and need to ride back in the dark. And I must – order the gig."

Eugenia considered. "Yes. You do all that, Bridget, and then we will go. I am sure I shall feel better at '*Paragon*'."

The two set out a half hour later.

It was strange how Eugenia's spirits did indeed lift as '*Paragon*' came into view. The cottage looked deserted, of course, being shut up while her mother was away, but it still represented all that had been happiest in Eugenia's life.

To Eugenia's surprise the key was not under the customary stone. Her mother must have been in such a hurry that she had forgotten to put it there when she left.

"You go on in," said Bridget encouragingly. "I'll tether the gig."

Inside '*Paragon*' the windows were half shuttered and the furniture shrouded. Yet in the half light of the drawing room, Eugenia felt that something was amiss. The room was not as cold as it should be, being unoccupied at this time of the year. Indeed, the ashes in the grate seemed warm. It was as if someone had been furtively living here.

"Little flower!"

Eugenia spun round at the sound of this oh, so familiar voice.

"Gregor!"

The painter, for indeed it was he, flung himself with a cry at her feet.

"Yes. It is I. Gregor Brodosky, who loves you, little treasure, to distraction. How my heart it dances in my breast to see you here."

Eugenia looked from Gregor to Bridget – who had appeared beaming at the door behind – in bewilderment.

"But what – what are you doing here? And why are you declaring yourself in this way now?"

"How could I declare myself in this way before?" he moaned. "What did you write to me? Nothing! What did you say to me? Nothing! You read my letters and put them away, that was all. I was sure you loved your Marquis. But now – now I know you are not happy and you are not happy because you love *me*, Gregor! Of this I am now sure. And because I am sure, I can DEMAND that you leave him and come with me."

Eugenia was shocked. "I – cannot. I am married to him."

"But, little flower, it is *not consummated*," roared Gregor.

Eugenia gasped and cast accusing eyes at Bridget.

"I had to tell him, my Lady!" Bridget blurted out. "Otherwise he would never have thought to come for you. See, if your marriage is not consummated, you can get it annulled."

Eugenia put her hands to her head. "I – I can?"

"Yes! So come with me now, today." urged Gregor. "To Europe we will fly and begin there a new life. When your marriage is annulled, we will marry."

Eugenia felt dizzy. Passion was being offered to her, passion and adventure. It was all she had ever dreamed of. Yet still she hesitated, her brow creased.

"But – I could never treat the Marquis so – shabbily."

Gregor and Bridget glanced at each other.

"Why not?" demanded Bridget. "When he treats you so shabbily as to take a mistress, right under your nose!"

Eugenia blenched and started back. "L-lady Walling?"

"That's right." Bridget looked triumphant. "And it's been going on for longer than you think. So come away, my Lady. I'll be your chaperone until such time as – you are free to marry Gregor. I'll look after you, you don't have to worry."

"I have – nothing with me," pleaded Eugenia.

Bridget gave a laugh. "You've got your jewels, my Lady. I made certain of that. I've got them in the gig, in a leather pouch."

Eugenia looked troubled.

"I am not sure this is the right thing to do," she began, but Gregor cut her short, grasping her to his breast and planting such a hard kiss on her lips that she could barely breathe. Her senses reeled. This, this was the fever of desire that Bridget had so colourfully described.

She was won! She buried her head against Gregor's breast as he swept her up into his arms and carried her to the door. Bridget hurried ahead to untie the horses and ready the gig. As the wheels ground into the mud and the horses leapt forward under the crack of her whip, the heavens split open and heavy, storm-charged rain began to fall.

CHAPTER NINE

Eugenia stirred uneasily and opened her eyes.

She lay under rough blankets in a small bedroom with leaded windows and exposed rafters. The room was neat enough but bare with the bed and a wooden chest the only furniture.

She raised her hand to her forehand, trying to remember the sequence of events that had brought her here. It was something of an effort, because her mind felt curiously unfocused.

She recalled a mad dash through the rain before arriving at a single story cottage. Whether the appearance of this cottage was fortuitous or expected she could not say as she was so cold and tired. That there was food to eat was not a surprise, since Bridget had suggested bringing 'refreshment' for the visit to '*Paragon*', although the *quantity* was a surprise – a whole game pie, a chicken, bread and apples.

Bridget immediately set about laying the table, while Gregor occupied himself building a fire in the grate. Eugenia sat shivering in a corner, watching the man for whom she had jettisoned her honour and position in Society. He ignored her, intent on his task. When the fire was lit he beckoned her over.

She sat on a stool while he poured a kind of punch

from a flask that he carried at his belt. Soon after drinking, Eugenia felt sleepy, so sleepy that she barely remembered eating. Later, someone had carried her to bed.

Bridget must have undressed her, for she was in her shift.

Hearing voices from beyond the chamber door, she realised what had awakened her.

She climbed out of bed, crossed the floor barefoot and opened the door.

In the room beyond, Bridget and Gregor sat at a table, on which lay Eugenia's jewellery in a heap. She recognised the pearls that Great-Aunt Cloris had given her, as well as many pieces that were gifts from the Marquis, including a ruby brooch and ear-rings, a turquoise bracelet and a diamond necklace. The diamonds sparkled in the shaft of winter light that fell through the window.

Eugenia was horrified to see, amid the spoils, a ring with the Buckbury seal. The Marquis had entrusted this emblem of his family to his fiancée and its presence here felt like theft. Bridget should not have taken it!

In fact, the removal of each piece of jewellery felt like theft.

"We must take it all back," she cried from the doorway.

Bridget and Gregor looked up with a start.

"If I have left my husband, then I must leave him all that he gave me," she continued.

Gregor looked incredulous. "What – have I saddled myself with a fool?"

Eugenia drew back, stung beyond measure by his tone. "A f-fool? What have I said that you should be so discourteous?"

Gregor was about to reply angrily when Bridget threw

him a warning glance. Eugenia might have dwelt more on this signal of complicity between the two of them, but that Gregor, curbing his temper, rose and came to her. Close to, his green eyes bored into hers.

"What are you doing out of bed?" he murmured. "You will catch cold, my *jewel*."

Eugenia blinked at being called "jewel".

"What *kind* of jewel am I?" she asked with a faint attempt at defusing the tension that she sensed within him.

"What kind?" Gregor considered. "I think you are – a pearl. Yes. That pink flush – that translucence." He sank his fingers into her loose mane of hair and pressed so close that she felt she would melt at his heat.

"You are my pearl and that is why you must listen to me and obey me and not be a silly little fool. The money from the portraits I have painted will soon be gone. We need to sell this jewellery, for how else will we live?"

"Why, you – you can paint!" said Eugenia.

Gregor snorted. "Paint? What do I make from that? Enough to breathe until the next painting. And then one day there are no more commissions and I starve. Always I must bow and kiss the ground beneath the feet of people who do not understand my great talent."

"You are going to stop – being an artist?" gulped Eugenia.

Gregor shrugged. "Probably not. But in France or Holland I will paint *when* I like and, more important, *who* I like."

Bridget placed a stool before the fire and took Eugenia's wool cape from where it had been drying on the back of a chair.

"Here. Wrap that round you, miss. I'll make your breakfast."

Eugenia took the cape, noting that Bridget had reverted to addressing her as 'miss' rather than 'my Lady'. Well, what could she expect? Had she not herself abdicated the role of Marchioness? She was once again plain Miss Eugenia!

She drew the cape around her with a shiver. She did not want to think about the Marquis. Her future lay with Gregor. As soon as she was divorced she would be his wife, as she had always dreamed of being.

She would have liked to see her mother's reaction then!

Mrs. Brodosky. Mrs. Brodosky. Eugenia tried out the name silently.

Bridget handed her a bowl of tea and set a plate of bread at her feet. She took the refreshments gratefully, warming her hands around the cup.

"Bridget?"

"Yes, miss?"

"What is this – place?"

"Don't rightly know, miss. It was a blessing to find it last night. We didn't want to take the London road, see, and were taking a short cut through some woods. But it was getting late and the weather was something awful. I think we're about thirty miles from – "

Gregor interrupted sharply. "Bridget, you talk too much."

"Yes, Gregor," Bridget chuckled. "I do."

Eugenia wondered at this effect of Gregor on her maid. She twisted round on her stool to look at her beloved. He was sitting again at the table, holding an emerald brooch – one she had not noticed earlier – to his eye.

"Green as the Volga," he murmured.

Eugenia felt suddenly lost and helpless. She longed

for a kind word or an embrace from Gregor. If only he would look at her, smile at her. She had always understood him to be an artist, someone who cared nothing for material things. Yet now he seemed more interested in these – these stones – than in the woman who had given up everything to be with him.

Gregor became aware of her longing gaze. "Do not worry about your jewels. They will buy us all a new life. Now, you must finish your breakfast."

"Bridget," she asked, rising from the stool, "where is my dress?"

Bridget looked shifty. "What do you want that for, miss?"

"Why – I must get ready to leave."

There was a silence. Bridget glanced at Gregor. "Leave, miss?"

Eugenia's brow creased. "Surely – we are moving on today?"

Gregor growled an answer from the table. "We are going nowhere. We have business to finish. We might as well finish it here as anywhere else."

Eugenia looked in puzzlement from Gregor to Bridget and back. "What kind of business?"

With an exclamation Gregor leaped to his feet, in the process scattering some of the jewellery from the table.

"Business that is none of your business! Do you think you are your 'ladyship' here that you torment me with questions?"

Bridget, scrambling on her knees to retrieve the pieces of jewellery, looked up.

"I'd go back to your room, miss, if I were you."

"Yes, Bridget. Yes, I will."

Eugenia stumbled to her room, closed the door behind

her and sank onto the bed. She had known Gregor was mercurial but these shifts of mood were like nothing she had experienced. More than anything in the world, she longed for the return of the lover she had imagined Gregor to be.

As if in answer to her prayers, the door opened and Gregor appeared.

"You are crying, little flower?"

Eugenia faced him squarely. "No."

"Good. Crying I do not like. And I do not like too many questions. That is not what your lips are for. Your lips are for – this."

His kiss was rough and prolonged and soon her head began to swim. She did not know if this was due to passion or lack of breath. Then Gregor pulled away and brushed back a lock of his hair.

"Better you stay in your room now," he ordered. "Then you do not make me angry."

"Yes, Gregor," Eugenia heard herself whispering.

She was ashamed of her timidity but the loneliness of her situation had suddenly struck her with great force. She had given her life over to this man. She had no one else in the world now, for not only had she foresworn her husband, she had by her flight estranged herself from her mother and great-aunt as well. Neither they nor Society could welcome her back after her behaviour. That the Marquis had a mistress would not be considered just cause for her to so abandon her duties.

Towards noon, Bridget brought her food and a bowl to wash in. When Eugenia again demanded her clothes, Bridget shook her head.

"He doesn't want you to have them, miss."

Eugenia was perplexed. "But why?"

Bridget shrugged. "Orders, miss."

Eugenia stared at her. She wondered what Bridget's role could be in this whole affair.

Hearing the sound of wheels, she jumped up and ran to the window, only to see Gregor in the gig disappearing through the trees.

"Where is he going?" she demanded of Bridget.

"Like he said, business," replied Bridget mysteriously.

Gregor returned at dusk. He did not come in to see Eugenia. She yearned to see him, despite his kaleidoscopic temper. Indeed, perhaps *because* of this same temper, her desire for his favour was increasing the more precarious that favour seemed.

Yet it was not of Gregor that she dreamed that night, but of the Marquis. Her erstwhile husband was carrying her through a torrent of wild water, a flood that threatened both their lives.

A whole day and evening passed followed by another day. Gregor came in and out to see her but he seemed on tenterhooks, crossing endlessly to the window as if watching for a visitor.

Eugenia dared not question him, for that would risk his displeasure. She was grateful for every crumb of tenderness he threw her way, although she began to suspect that these exhibitions of affection were prompted rather than felt. He seemed to be doing what was necessary to maintain her interest in him without taxing the limits of his own interest in her. This from the man who two days previously had vehemently declaimed his love for her!

At last she could restrain her feelings no longer. As he paced the floor of her room, she summoned up the courage necessary to confront him.

"I want to know," she ventured, "why you made me run away with you when you – when you now do not seem to care for me at all. Why are you keeping me a prisoner

137

here? What do you hope to gain from me? I have abandoned everything and I have no money. Only the jewels, and those you have in your possession already – "

Her breath ran out.

When she had begun to speak, Gregor had halted in his tracks and now he stood in the shadows. She could hear his breathing and for a moment she felt as if an animal was waiting to pounce.

"G-Gregor?" she prompted.

He emerged from the shadows. She drew back on the bed, pulling her shift down over her knees and observing her, he gave a short laugh.

"Oh, you think I want to steal your virtue? What a story you live in. The romantic heroine, who loves the wild artist, who throws everything away for him. Well I will tell you. Everything you threw away, I want. Not the Marquis naturally but – his wealth, his power, his house, his land. If I could have all that, I would never care to see a paint brush again.

"As for you – why should I take what the Marquis himself would not take? I have other designs, other plans, which you will know about soon."

Eugenia listened in mounting horror. She understood at last that this was not the passionate artist she had believed she loved. What she had taken to be the diffidence of one whose interests were of a higher order was nothing more than capricious cruelty.

It had taken less than three days of his company for the veil to fall from her eyes.

*

Later that evening Bridget brought a bowl of soup. The maid seemed uneasy and unwilling to engage in conversation, although she kept Eugenia company while she ate. As Eugenia laid her spoon down, there came the sound of hooves from without.

Bridget twisted her hands together. "He's come, then," she mumbled.

"Who?" asked Eugenia but her voice was drowned by the sound of hammering at the door. She heard Gregor respond and the visitor stepped in. He spoke, and Eugenia's heart nearly ceased to beat.

It was her husband, the Marquis.

Hearing him, such relief swept over her that she realised, almost with dismay, that she had been longing to hear his voice since the moment she had set foot in this cottage.

Sure that he had come for her, she leapt to her feet and rushed to the door, only to have Bridget step resolutely in her way. She opened her mouth to cry out but Bridget raised a warning finger to her lips.

"I know what you're thinking, miss, but you're wrong. He hasn't come to fetch you home. He doesn't even know you're here. He's come as Gregor bid him to do business. He wouldn't have you back now for all the rubies in the world. Not after you've spent these nights here with Gregor. And you still in your shift!"

Eugenia staggered as she understood.

If she attempted to make her presence known to the Marquis, how would it look to see her barefoot and in her shift, with her hair tangled and loose upon her shoulders? It would only compound for him the impression that Bridget had hinted at – that Eugenia and Gregor had become lovers. An impression Gregor, for reasons of his own, had no doubt encouraged.

"Can I not – at least see him?" she pleaded with Bridget.

Bridget looked askance. "And three days ago you

wanted nothing more to do with him! You don't know your own mind, miss."

Eugenia knew this to be so bitterly true that there was no answer. She leaned her forehead against the door, listening, while Bridget sauntered to the bed and sat down, confident now that her charge would not reveal herself at any price.

Eugenia could hear the two men conversing. Gregor was playing the host, offering tea and a seat by the fire. The Marquis declined both.

"You have summoned me here for what you call business reasons," Eugenia heard him say. "So let us not waste time on common courtesies."

Such a burning desire to look upon her husband's face came over Eugenia that she threw what caution she had to the wind. Stealing a glance at Bridget, who now lay prone on the bed humming and staring at the rafters, she edged the door open and peered through the chink.

Gregor sat sprawled in a chair before the fire. The Marquis stood, gloves in hand, on the other side of the hearth. The firelight flickered over his resolute features.

"Well?" he demanded of Gregor. "Perhaps you would like to begin by giving me news of my wife."

"She is well, she eats heartily, she sleeps – like a contented lamb," replied Gregor, crossing one leg over the other and staring up insolently at the Marquis.

The Marquis clenched his jaw. "Where does she sleep, you rogue? Here, in this dog kennel of a place?"

"Oh," answered Gregor jauntily, "I will do better than this for her, if we come to an agreement."

The Marquis glowered. "What kind of agreement do you propose?"

Gregor sat up, uncrossing his leg and leaning forward

with an intent gaze. "First, *I* put some questions to *you*. Is it a concern of yours, what they call here '*family honour*'?"

"As concerned as any Englishman," responded the Marquis shortly.

"And you are concerned also with your reputation?"

The Marquis gave a laugh of derision. "Reputation? Surely a concept foreign to your nature, Brodosky."

"Nevertheless," Gregor persisted coolly, "there are certain facts regarding – how do you call it? – your conjugal relations – that no sane man would wish to be made common knowledge."

Eugenia felt faint with horror. Gregor's inference was clear to her and she knew that it was equally clear to the Marquis.

"By Heaven, you tread on dangerous ground," her husband said softly. "May I ask how you came to be privy to – the information at which you hint?"

"Certainly," replied Gregor with a monstrous smile. "I heard it from your wife's own lips – along with her kisses."

Eugenia closed her eyes in dismay. How was the Marquis to know that Gregor was lying?

The Marquis stood very still. His voice when he spoke was as ice.

"What is it you want?"

Gregor turned and spat into the fire. "Your wife has become used to luxury. She wants to keep, for example, her lady's maid. I will need money to keep her – *Ladyship* – in the style she expects."

The Marquis looked stony. "Go on."

Gregor shrugged. "It is simple. Settle a sum of money on her for life. Or the details of your – unconsummated marriage – will somehow find their way into the public ear."

The Marquis clenched his fists at his side – one hand

still holding his gloves – but if he was tempted to strike Gregor, he thought better of it.

"Did my wife plan this pretty scheme with you?"

Gregor stretched his arms above his head and yawned. "Your wife? She has not the taste for this kind of matter."

Eugenia was grateful that at least Gregor had not implicated her. Her gratitude was quickly dispelled, however, by Gregor's next remark.

"Why not pay up and be done with it? What will Society know of the affair? Only that your wife ran away with a painter. *She* will be the guilty party."

The Marquis turned and regarded Gregor narrowly.

"My wife is unconcerned that her name be thus sullied?"

"Correct."

"And she will not see me to tell me this herself?"

"Correct."

The Marquis crossed to the window and looked out at the wood. His back now turned completely from the room, Eugenia felt emboldened to open the door a little wider and peer out at him. His tall, upright figure was outlined against the moonlit glass, his head thrown back as if contemplating the night sky.

Eugenia followed his gaze. Stars glittered sharply, like thousands of minute diamonds. Like the diamonds the Marquis himself had given her, out of love, sheer love. The diamonds that Bridget had then taken to finance their flight.

'Oh,' thought Eugenia, '*what a callous fool I have been*!' She leaned against the doorjamb, sick with guilt and shame.

The Marquis gave a sigh.

"What sum do you propose, Brodosky?" he asked in a dull voice.

Gregor gave a sneer. "How much do you value your reputation?"

The Marquis turned and regarded Gregor with distaste. "It is rather a question of how much I value my wife."

Eugenia did not draw back from the door as she should have, but stood as if mesmerised by this clear sight of her husband's face. She was struck by the nobility she detected.

Gregor was looking at the Marquis with curiosity. "What, you concern yourself with a woman who does not care for you?"

"I would wish no woman connected to me in any way, sir, to sink into a life of poverty."

Gregor looked amused. "Such principles! Well, maybe they should cost you – about five thousand pounds, say?"

Eugenia gulped silently at the amount but the Marquis did not flinch.

"Five thousand it is," he said.

How easily he agreed, thought Eugenia with dismay, drawing back into the shadows. She felt deeply, irrationally wounded that her husband was so willing to let her go. He must indeed be heavily involved with Lady Walling.

"I presume you will be expecting me to file for a divorce," continued the Marquis. "So that you are free to marry – Eugenia."

"Oh, certainly, certainly," returned Gregor quickly. "But – as regards the matter in hand. How do you intend to pay me?"

The Marquis began to draw on his gloves. "You said you were taking – my wife – abroad?"

"To Amsterdam. Or Paris," replied Gregor cautiously.

"Let it be Paris," said the Marquis. "The money will

be deposited in monthly instalments at the Bank de Cluny in the Rue Demareille."

Gregor looked disappointed. *"Monthly instalments?"*

The Marquis was firm. "Yes."

Gregor had obviously hoped for a lump sum.

"In *my* name, then," he proposed at last.

The Marquis's response was quick and steely. "In my *wife's* name, sir."

Sullenly, Gregor agreed. "You wish to tie me to her apron strings!"

"Exactly!" said the Marquis.

He turned to leave and Eugenia's heart plummeted. She had not understood the last part of the exchange nor what it imported. Her mind had begun to swim with despair as she realised that this might be the last time she ever set eyes on the Marquis. Once she had sought to flee from him, now she could not bear to see him go. Out of her sight, out of her life, this man whose worth she was only now beginning to appreciate.

All caution left her. With a cry she threw wide the bedroom door and rushed out.

"My Lord!"

He stiffened and slowly turned. His eyes ran up and down her body, registering the shift, the exposed flesh where it had slipped from her shoulder, the bare legs and feet, the tousled mane. Then he lifted his gaze to her face. Her stricken expression appeared to move him not one jot, for he accorded her nothing more than a polite bow.

"Madam," he said, and was gone.

Eugenia walked unsteadily to the table and, sinking into a chair, buried her head in her hands.

Gregor prodded her shoulder jeeringly.

"I knew you'd be the fool enough to show yourself

eventually. Just what I wanted! The way you look, if he was not sure that you had given yourself to me, he is now."

Eugenia lifted her head dazedly, just as Bridget came dancing out of the bedroom.

"Five thousand pounds!" Bridget crowed. "We'll live like Kings!"

Gregor threw back his head and laughed like a madman. He grasped Bridget about the waist and whirled her into the air.

Eugenia watched in disbelief as the two of them pranced in triumph about the room.

"Five thousand, five thousand, a merry five thousand," they sang.

It was clear at last to Eugenia that these two had been in league for some time. She dug her fingers into her hair, full of anguish. Gregor had no feeling for her and Bridget had betrayed her. They surely had no desire to have her remain in their company.

Not for one moment did Eugenia entertain the belief that the Marquis's decision to pay was purely the result of self-interest or that he feared his honour would be stained by the public revelation that he had not consummated his marriage. She felt, at last, that she knew him better than that.

Gregor and Bridget, finally out of breath, threw themselves onto the wooden settle that stood against the far wall and stared at Eugenia. She felt that they, too, were assessing the future they now faced – comfortable but in some way constrained, since she was their companion forever. Or, she thought with a sudden shiver, until the money runs out!

Five thousand pounds was a great deal, certainly, but it would not last a lifetime. Perhaps Gregor intended to repeat his threat of blackmail at some time in the future. He could always taunt the Marquis with visions of Eugenia becoming poor and down at heel. Or would the Marquis, once he was divorced, wash his hands of his former wife and consider her fate to be none of his business?

Bridget, recovered from her exertions, got up and came over to Eugenia.

"Don't look so glum, miss. We can all have a good time together, can't we, Gregor?"

Gregor rose and spat into the fire again. "Certainly we can."

Bridget stroked Eugenia's hair. "You thought you had it all, didn't you, miss? But it's me who's got it all now. I'm the rich one now. I'm the pretty one."

Eugenia had to agree that Bridget did indeed look pretty. Her skin was rosy, her eyes sparkled, her lips glistened like rosehips touched with dew. This was the effect of love, no doubt.

"You care – so much for him?" she asked, indicating Gregor.

Bridget's eyes strayed fondly to where the painter stood, prodding an unburned log in the hearth with his boot.

"He's a card, miss," was all she replied.

Gregor grunted. Almost as if he sensed Eugenia's eyes on his back he turned and gave her an unexpected wink.

"We will all get along like old friends," he said. " Why not, little flower?"

Disgust curdled in Eugenia like spoiled milk. Disgust at Gregor, disgust at herself. From here unto eternity she must live with the bitter knowledge that she had been an almighty fool.

She had thrown away her whole life for nothing more than a fantasy.

CHAPTER TEN

The sea lapped in the dark, like a dog at a trough.   A gull wheeled in the inky air, hoping for a stray crust, though most of the craft in the harbour bore no lights.   It was an eerily silent scene.

Eugenia shivered as she stood waiting on the quayside. A chill wind snapped at the brim of her bonnet – or rather, Bridget's bonnet.   Gregor had decided that Eugenia should not look too much of a lady as they travelled.   For some reason he was nervous of attracting attention.   Eugenia did not understand this, since nobody was chasing after her.

Perhaps it was simply in Gregor's nature to feel hunted.

Bridget had happily yielded up her plain brown bonnet and her worsted cape.   In return, she wore Eugenia's woollen cloak with its warm hood.   It made her feel like a Duchess, she said.

Eugenia had been grateful for the ensuing silence.   The exchange had taken place in the coach that had brought the three of them from the town of Ipswich, where they had sold the gig and horses, to this seaport on the east coast.   She had been tired and only wanted to sleep, her head against the musty upholstery.

But whenever she closed her eyes she was confronted with the image of the Marquis, his features as she had last seen him, inexpressive as stone.

The coach had arrived at the harbour just as night was drawing in. With the money from the sale, Gregor had treated them all to supper at the *Seaman's Tavern*.

"Maybe this is our last meal until the Marquis deposits the money!" he declared, gnawing on a ham bone.

Now Gregor and Bridget had gone off to find someone who would agree to row them out to the French frigate, whose lights twinkled beyond the mouth of the harbour.

Eugenia shivered again and drew the cape about her. She had been alone here for nigh on an hour. Suppose something had happened to her companions?

She heard the sound of a hatch being dragged open and saw a man emerge onto the deck of a fishing boat. She watched him empty a bucket of slops into the water.

When next she glanced out to sea she gave a start. Creeping in from the harbour mouth came a grey, clammy fog. The lights of the French ship had disappeared.

Now Eugenia felt truly alone. The fog crept in and in until it wreathed about her. It smelled of salt and seaweed and, she imagined, the breath of those who had died in the cold waves.

She stiffened at the sound of footsteps.

"Gregor? Bridget?" she called hopefully.

How desolate she must be indeed when she yearned for the return of the very two creatures who had lured her into this abysmal situation!

Someone stood for a moment, as if listening. She thought she made out the glow of a lantern not far off. Before she could move towards it her arm was seized and she was dragged without ceremony in the opposite direction.

"I told you to wait by the jetty," Gregor hissed into her ear.

Eugenia regarded him nervously. He was swaying like

a weathercock and both he and Bridget, who was at his elbow, reeked of gin.

"I did," she replied. "But I grew cold and walked to keep myself warm. Did you – did you find anyone to row us out?"

Gregor scowled. "It would have been easier to find the devil! They're too fond of the fireside in this backwater. I did find a boat though."

Eugenia swallowed. "Y-you are going to row?"

"Yes. Why not?"

Eugenia did not want to comment on his inebriated state. "You – you don't know these waters, and there's a fog."

Gregor turned his wavering gaze to the sea. "I can see there's a fog! But once beyond the harbour, we can hail the frigate. They will show a lantern for us."

"Suppose they don't want to take us on board?" fretted Bridget.

Gregor drew a money pouch from his pocket and rattled it. "We've got enough left here to convince them. They will take us."

The boat he had found for their escape looked very flimsy, bobbing up and down at the foot of the jetty steps.

The boat rocked wildly as she and Bridget stepped in. Gregor cast off the rope and climbed in after them. He took up the oars and began to row.

Soon the lights of the shore had vanished. Nothing existed but fog. It felt to Eugenia as if she was travelling through layers of cobweb. A damp, soft cobweb, that trailed across her face. All sound was muted, even Gregor's harsh breath. His face, and Bridget's face, seemed to loom in the air, detached from their physical bodies.

The two women sat with their skirts lifted to their calves. Water slopped about their ankles and the boat smelled of fish. With that and the wafts of gin-soaked breath that came from Gregor and Bridget, Eugenia began to feel queasy.

Bridget peered over the edge. "Ooh, that water's black as pitch. I shouldn't like to fall in, I shouldn't."

"Nor I," shuddered Eugenia.

Gregor's eyes shifted to her and some wicked thought gleamed in their depths.

"Do you swim, Bridget?" he asked.

"Not I!" Bridget exclaimed. "I lived right by the river Thames when I was a girl, but it never tempted me. You don't know what's in it, do you? There was all kinds of filth. My brother used to catch fish and when he brought them home their scales was the colour of dirty linen. My stepfather wouldn't touch them. The sea looks a bit cleaner but I don't trust it. Imagine all those sailors who've died."

Eugenia had never known Bridget so voluble. She supposed it was the gin.

"Can you swim, Gregor?" she heard Bridget ask.

Gregor shook his head. "It must be Eugenia who will save us if we sink!" he said with an apparent attempt at jocularity.

Eugenia gave a weak smile. "Well, then, we would all drown, for I cannot swim a stroke."

"That is unfortunate," Gregor murmured, an unpleasant smile lurking on his lips.

He lowered his head to the oars and gave such a pull that the boat gave a harsh lurch forward. Eugenia and Bridget were thrown about on their wooden bench.

"Steady on!" cried Bridget.

Gregor laboured fiercely. He laboured as if a pack of hounds was at his heels. The veins in his temples stood out and his chest heaved with effort.

"Must get – out of the harbour," he panted. "Must get – on."

Eugenia wondered how far they were now from the quay. The temperature was dropping and she began to shiver.

"Quiet!" warned Gregor.

They all fell silent. Eugenia heard, faintly and at some distance, the slap of another prow against water.

Gregor cursed under his breath.

"Who else is out here with us, who?"

They waited. The sound of the other boat faded away and Gregor took up the oars again. His rowing seemed more urgent than ever. Eugenia could not look at him. The face she had once thought so handsome and so alluring, she now found mean and cruel.

Since the Marquis had walked out of that cottage deep in the woods, Eugenia felt she had changed profoundly. She had been set upon the bitter rack of experience and it had stretched her soul beyond endurance. Yet endure she must and endure she would.

The only alternative would be to take a step that was forbidden by law and forbidden by faith. She knew all about those poor unfortunate suicides buried outside the churchyard walls, beyond the comfort of religion. She would not travel that road, tempting though it was to her in her profound misery.

She would find some way of leading a life of value. Perhaps she could teach on the Continent. She did not believe that Gregor would raise objections to her contributing to the household in such a way. She was certain now he had no intention of marrying her and she was equally certain that he had no interest in seducing her. She was simply his ticket out of the impoverished life of an artist.

She did not believe he would marry Bridget either,

though she was sure Bridget would leap at the chance of marrying him.

Theirs was going to be a curious household, scrambled together in some apartment near the Bank de Cluny, where the Marquis would be depositing their funds.

She was suddenly aware that Gregor had stopped rowing. He was leaning on the oars and Bridget was wiping his streaming brow with the hem of her cloak.

"Bridget," he asked as the maid at last sat back. "Where are those jewels?"

"They're safe," said Bridget.

"Show me."

Bridget looked surprised. "Out here? What for?"

"Show me!" repeated Gregor with greater force.

Bridget withdrew a leather pouch from her cloak. "Here they are."

"Open it," ordered Gregor. "I want to be sure everything is there. I remember some pieces falling to the floor – back there – in the cottage."

"I picked them all up," Bridget pointed out.

"I want to be sure!" Gregor insisted. "There is one piece in particular – the ring with the Buckbury seal – "

Bridget felt in the bag. "It's here."

"Good." Gregor seemed more than satisfied. A peculiar hue shone in his eyes, a hue suggesting a greater darkness in his soul than had hitherto been manifest.

Bridget took the ring out and polished it on her sleeve.

"It's nice," she said. "I'd like to keep this. *If* you don't mind," she added, turning to Eugenia in mock courtesy.

"I no longer have the right to wear it," replied Eugenia dully. She turned her head as she thought she heard the dipping of an oar through the waves. That other boat again!

Bridget slipped the ring onto her finger. "Now *I'm* the Marchioness!" she crowed.

"That's it!" cried Gregor, leaning heavily on the oars. "You understand!"

"I do?" Bridget, stalled in her triumph, looked perplexedly from Eugenia to Gregor.

"With that ring," Gregor pointed," you enter the bank in Paris and if you say you are the Marchioness of Buckbury, they will believe you. You will be able to draw out the money that the Marquis deposits there every month."

"But why should I, when *she's* there to do it?" asked Bridget, indicating Eugenia.

Eugenia, beginning to understand the direction that Gregor's thoughts were taking, tremblingly answered for him,

"*But if I was not?*"

Gregor regarded her with a chilling laugh. "Bravo, little flower. At last you understand the story."

"*She* might, *I* don't," grumbled Bridget.

"If anything should happen to me, you would be able to continue drawing the money," said Eugenia, trying not to show her growing fear, "and no one would ever know."

Gregor clapped his hands. "That's it! You see, Bridget, how hard it has been for me to row with three people in the boat. Such weight! You see – my palms already begin to blister."

"That's terrible, Gregor!" clucked Bridget. "Let me tear the hem off the cloak and bind them for you – "

Impatiently, Gregor brushed away her hands.

"Listen. *Listen!* It's going to be even harder than this rowing has been to drag three people around the Continent for the rest of our lives. We will be manacled to her and think – five thousand pounds will go much further if there are only two of us!"

Bridget, searching his face, suddenly shrank into her cloak. "I don't know about that – "

But Gregor silenced her with a wave of his hand. "What do you think about this idea, little flower?" he asked Eugenia jeeringly.

"I wonder that it did not occur to you earlier," replied Eugenia, feigning calm. "But – as a matter of curiosity – why me and not Bridget?"

Gregor threw back his head. "You – ha ha ha – I do not trust and do not desire. You I could crack too easily – like an eggshell – *she* can take rough treatment. Ha ha ha."

Eugenia thought that she had succeeded in playing for time, but Gregor's next move took her completely by surprise. With a roar he leapt up, dragged her to her feet, and made as if to fling her overboard.

Unprepared as she was, she struggled. She heard Bridget screeching as the boat rocked to and fro and water splashed over the stern. Her hand flailed in the air before it caught hold of Gregor's jacket and held on tight.

She was falling, falling, and he was falling too. With a terrible cry she hit the water.

She gasped at the cold, went under, surfaced and went under again. She kicked with her heels and came up for a second time. She caught a glimpse of Gregor, foundering nearby. And Bridget, taking up the oars of the boat.

Salt stung her eyes and she began to sink. Her skirt and petticoat, heavier by the second, ballooned about her. This was the end! The end!

Darkness began to descend on her mind –

Two arms reached down through the water. Two arms clasped themselves firmly about her waist. Two arms – tender, strong and determined – drew her barely conscious from the greedy embrace of the sea.

*

A soft wind sang in the chimney at '*Paragon.*' Eugenia held out her hands to the flames. She was not cold but the dancing fire seemed to draw her to its heart. Apart from the wind and the crackle of logs in the grate, the house was quiet. Beyond the windows, the treetops swayed gently to and fro but made no murmur. She was alone. Alone with her thoughts and they, alas, were unsettling company.

After her rescue from the sea she had known nothing more until she had awakened at dawn in a room at the *Sailor's Tavern*. The first face she saw before her was that of the Marquis.

It was he, she discovered, who had saved her.

"Y-you were in the boat we heard in the distance?"

"Yes."

Although the Marquis had been watching her intently when she had first woken, now he seemed reluctant to talk to her. He rose and began to pace the room.

Eugenia followed him with her eyes. "Why? Why were you there at all? I do not understand. When you left the cottage you – you were returning to Buckbury, surely?"

The Marquis halted at the window.

"I did not go to Buckbury," he said shortly. "I rode to the nearest town and found two officers of the law. You see, when Brodosky tried to get me to deposit the – money – in his name, I was instantly suspicious, although I did my best to conceal it. I feared for your safety."

"Y-you did?"

"As I would for the safety of any woman in such a situation," said the Marquis coldly, as if to forestall any hope she might harbour of regaining his affections. He resumed his pacing. "I returned with the officers to the cottage, intending to snatch you from Brodosky's clutches, only to find the place empty.

"Guessing that he would head immediately for the nearest port from which to travel to France, I followed. The officers accompanied me. At the port we separated, each searching a different area of town. We soon learned Brodosky had been asking around for someone to row him out to the frigate.

"We were not sure from which direction he would approach the vessel, so we took a boat ourselves and waited at the harbour mouth, hoping to apprehend him there. Then the fog rolled in. It was a mercy that we came upon you when we did."

"Yes," Eugenia agreed humbly. She hesitated before posing the next question,

"And did you – apprehend him?"

The Marquis glanced her way sharply.

"No. He drowned."

Eugenia drew in her breath with shock. Then, without warning, her eyes filled with tears.

She mourned for Gregor's folly, as well as her own, but the Marquis did not know that. His features hardened.

"I see, madam, that you grieve," he remarked stiffly.

Eugenia wiped away a tear that had begun to trickle down her cheek. "Not as you imagine, my Lord."

"What I imagine is of no consequence," remarked the Marquis, turning once again to the window and staring out.

"What about – Bridget?" she asked.

"In the chaos of the moment, she took up the oars and rowed swiftly from the scene. Neither she nor the jewels – oh, yes, I suspected that she had taken the jewels – have been found."

Eugenia realised that this was all the information she was going to receive. The Marquis may have saved her life, but he was not about to forgive her. She longed for his embrace, longed for the ardour he had once shown, but he was as distant to her now as a King to a common subject.

What could she expect? He was certain that she had – given herself up to Gregor, body and soul. If she tried to tell him the truth, he would not believe her. It would seem mere opportunism, now that Gregor was dead and she was without a protector of any kind.

Besides, there was the vexed question of Lady Walling.

Eugenia was sure that it was her own shameful behaviour that had caused the Marquis to stray. Nevertheless, part of her that could not quite forgive her husband for so easily finding an alternative interest!

She did not know what was to become of her. Her habitual spirited opposition to her mother's wishes now seemed the conduct of another being entirely.

Perhaps her entire future was to be spent in a series of humble rooms like that at the *Sailor's Tavern*.

It was the Marquis who, as if hearing her thoughts, suggested that she return to '*Paragon*'. When she began to protest that it was out of the question, he silenced her with a severe look.

"Dress yourself and then come down to the inn courtyard," he said. "I will order a coach."

He had not spoken to her on the journey, except to exchange common courtesies, or ask her if she wished him to halt the coach so that she might take refreshment of some kind.

He made no mention at all of what her future might entail until he handed her from the coach outside her beloved cottage. Then, drawing her out of earshot of his coachman, he told her what he had decided.

"Here you may live," he said. "I will continue to provide for you, but I desire no further communication between us. Explain it to your mother as you will. I shall never breathe a word of what has passed regarding yourself and Brodosky. Your reputation, as far as that adventure goes, is safe. You are at liberty to invent another reason for our – estrangement."

"Lady Walling, perhaps?" murmured Eugenia bitterly, close to tears.

"What do you mean by that?"

Eugenia bit her lip. "Nothing, my L-Lord."

"I am not your Lord anymore, Eugenia. I am nothing to you from now on and you are nothing to me."

He turned and strode back to the coach. Eugenia stood outside until the sound of the wheels faded in the dusky air. Then she opened the door of '*Paragon*' and went inside.

*

That had been two days ago. Two days! The most lonely of her life, her only companions the owls and wood pigeons that lived in the woods. She did not even have her old pony Bud, since he was now stabled at Buckbury and she did not dare approach the Abbey for fear the Marquis might see her.

She turned her head at the sound of a light knock.

The knocking continued, with increasing urgency. At last she walked to the door and cautiously opened it a crack. She peered out and then stepped back in astonishment. Bridget pushed the door wide and stared in.

"I had to see you, miss. It's important."

She looked exhausted and very bedraggled. Her stockings were torn and the hem of her dress trailed in the dust. She seemed to have lost Eugenia's woollen cloak. Eugenia took all this in and then motioned for her to enter.

With a look of relief, Bridget slipped into the house. She followed Eugenia to the drawing room and sank with a moan onto the sofa. Eugenia looked at her for a moment and then went to the kitchen, returning with bread and jam and a mug of ale. Bridget fell on the food hungrily.

"Thank you, miss, oh, thank you. I'm that grateful, I really am. I don't deserve it."

"No," agreed Eugenia candidly. "You do not."

She did not know why she was helping Bridget in this way. Perhaps she pitied her. After all, Gregor, the man she had loved, was dead.

"What do you want with me?" she asked Bridget at last.

Bridget took a swig of ale and then wiped her mouth on her sleeve.

"I wanted to return these, miss." She threw the leather pouch containing Eugenia's jewels onto the small table that stood before the sofa. "They're all there," she added.

Eugenia stared at the pouch. "What makes you give them up, Bridget? They would have fetched a lot of money – enough for you to start a new life somewhere and perhaps even become a lady."

Bridget burst into tears.

"I don't want to start a new life no more, miss. I don't want to be a lady. I just want to go back to London and look after Mrs. Dewitt like I used to. Before that Gregor came and turned my head! He used to taunt me about you, miss, even though he was making love to me."

Eugenia lowered her head with a bitter sigh. "Making love to you?"

"From the very first, miss. But – he'd flirt with you as he'd flirt with any creature that caught his eye and I got so jealous – I was glad when you and your mother left London for Buckbury. Then one day Gregor found out from your great-aunt that she was going to leave all her fortune to you and it set him thinking.

"He kept saying that your great-aunt was old and bound to die soon. If he could get you to marry him, he'd end up rich. I said I didn't want him to marry you, but he said not to be a fool, as once he had the money, he'd leave you and run off with me. He said I was – the right sort for him.

"He was impatient for you to return to London so that he might start his plan. Then Mrs. Dewitt received the invitation to visit you all. Gregor was thrilled, 'cos he knew she'd take me with her. And he made me promise that, once I got here, I was to set to work on you."

Eugenia raised her head. "Work on me?"

"Soften you up until he could get to you himself. Make you believe that – that he was in love with you. And I did it, even though half the time I didn't want to. Then you went and got yourself engaged. Even Gregor thought his plan was all over.

"And then came the commission to paint your portrait. He accepted 'cos he was sure he'd be able to get you to renounce the Marquis for him. But it didn't work out that way. After your marriage he really gave up.

"I didn't want to leave him, but you kept insisting that I go with you on your honeymoon. I could have killed you until – until I found out that you and the Marquis were not – not really man and wife after all. I wrote to Gregor and – and he replied, saying we had you now, he was sure of it. He decided to wait at '*Paragon*' until you were back, until such time as I thought you were – ripe."

"Ripe," repeated Eugenia in disbelief.

"Yes, miss. Miserable enough to leave your husband. Then I was to get you to '*Paragon*' and – and he'd do the rest. It worked. You came away." Bridget began to tug nervously at a strand of hair. "He told me we was going to abandon you once we'd got the money out of the Marquis. I never thought he'd do what he did, miss. Honest. I'd never have agreed to that, miss, never."

Eugenia nodded and then stared down at the pouch full of jewels. "And these?"

Bridget began to wail. "I don't want to hang for a string of pearl and some rings, miss. If I give them back, perhaps you'll put a word in for me with the Marquis and ask him not to press charges against me. Would you do that, miss?"

Eugenia pushed the pouch back towards Bridget. "I do not consider that they are mine to receive. And I no longer have the ear of the Marquis, for reasons which you must surely guess. You must go to him yourself and beg for mercy."

Bridget, sniffing, picked up the pouch. "Are you sure he will see me?" she asked doubtfully.

"I am sure he will," said Eugenia.

Bridget, somewhat fortified by the meal and ale, departed. Eugenia closed the door behind her but did not bolt it. She returned to the drawing room and sank into her chair before the fire, her mind in even greater turmoil. She had been nothing but a pawn in a game from the beginning, all the time believing she was experiencing a grand and illicit passion. Fool, fool, *fool*!

Apart from going to the kitchen to prepare herself some food, she spent the rest of the evening before the fire. She read, dropped the book onto her lap, took up some sewing and dropped it as well. Nothing could take her mind off the sorry tale that Bridget had told her.

It was getting on for midnight. The fire had begun to die, for she had not fed the flames for nearly an hour. The dying embers seemed to reflect her mood and she sat staring at them as if in a trance.

Only gradually did she become aware that someone

had entered the cottage. Had Bridget returned from her quest?

"W-who is there?" she called fearfully.

The Marquis stepped into the room from the corridor. Eugenia rose with a cry.

The Marquis apologised. "I am sorry to have startled you," he said. "I knocked but you did not hear. As the bolt was not drawn I made so bold as to enter."

His tone was considerably less severe than when they had last met and Eugenia felt bewildered.

"You said – you had no wish to communicate with me."

The Marquis nodded gravely. "Indeed I did. But – I received a visitor this afternoon who made me realise that you and I had – unfinished business."

Eugenia could not read his expression. "You mean Bridget?"

The Marquis inclined his head again. "Yes. I have agreed not to press charges."

"I am glad of that."

The Marquis regarded her, his head a little to one side. "I truly believe you are. Yes. You have a – generous if too impulsive heart."

"You have not come here to offer me guarded compliments, surely?"

"No. I – have items of yours that I thought I should return."

Eugenia began to feel alarmed. "What are they?"

"This is the first. This and its contents."

The Marquis withdrew an object from his waistcoat and threw it on the table. Eugenia froze. It was her reticule, in which lay the three letters that she had received from Gregor. She raised anguished eyes to the Marquis.

"You – you know what is inside?"

"I regret to say I do."

Trembling, Eugenia opened the reticule and withdrew the letters. She held them out in her fist to the Marquis. "You have – read them?"

"Madam, I – know what they – "

"That was – ungallant of you," she cried, taking him to mean he had indeed read them. "And it is ungallant, sir, to throw them at me now, when you have already pronounced sentence upon me. What further punishment do you wish to inflict?"

"I have not yet considered the matter of – punishment," murmured the Marquis.

Eugenia, breast heaving with anguish, lifted her chin. "You said that item was the first. What is the second?"

The Marquis hesitated. "I have it – in the corridor. I will bring it in."

Eugenia watched him as he left the room. Wracked with remorse and shame, she tightened her fist on the letters. The Marquis returned and as her eyes settled on the object he carried under his arm, the blood drained from her cheeks.

Although it was wrapped in a white cloth, she was sure that this was the portrait that Gregor had painted of her.

"I thought you would want it," said the Marquis simply.

She could bear his taunts no more. Rushing forward, she seized the canvas from him and, spinning on her heel, hurled it into what remained of the fire.

"You do not want to even look at it?" cried the Marquis.

"No. No. I do not. And I do not want to look at these either." Angrily she tossed the letters as well into the flickering tongues of flame. "I want nothing of that man, nothing. I do not want to remember him or what a fool I have made of myself. "

Taking up a poker, she stabbed at the portrait, trying to push it further down into the fire. Nothing would do but that it should be consumed to ashes. Once she was certain that it would indeed burn, she flung the poker aside and turned defiantly to the Marquis, who had stood silent all the while.

"So. Punish me then as you wish. I no longer care."

"No?" The Marquis strode forward and seized her roughly in his arms. "You do not care if I punish you – *thus*?"

She gasped as he plunged his fingers into her hair and, drawing back her head so that her face was tilted up to his, pressed furious kisses onto her lips.

"And thus – and thus – and thus – " he repeated.

"What are you doing?" she cried.

"I am taking what is mine!" the Marquis replied. "I have been half mad with jealousy since the moment I realised you were falling under the spell of another man. I thought patience and kindness would win you.

"I thought all would be well once we were married but your tears on our wedding night showed me otherwise. Then you ran away.

"My agony was intense. It was even more intense when I understood the character of the man for whom you had left me. The kind of man who I was sure would force you to his will as I should have forced you to mine.

"As I *will* force you, my darling."

With a groan he lowered his head once again to hers, taking her lip between his teeth until it bled.

A thrill swept through Eugenia's veins such as she had never experienced. As hard as the Marquis's heart pounded beneath his shirt, her heart pounded harder.

"M-my lord," she panted, falling against his breast.

"Yes, your Lord, Eugenia, as you are my Lady."

She looked up at him with troubled eyes.

"But – surely you are mocking me? How can you want me when you believe that – that I was – that man's creature?"

Struggling to restrain his passion, the Marquis held her face in his hands.

"I wronged you, my sweetheart. Bridget has told me all."

Eugenia began to tremble with relief. "All?"

"Yes. I longed to fly to you there and then. Only one fear held me back."

"What fear was that?" whispered Eugenia.

"That you were still in love with a dead man. I did not actually read his letters, my darling, but Bridget outlined their contents to me and I understood the force of his charm. It was all too likely that you still harboured a passion for him. Your reaction just now to those very letters – and to the portrait – convinced me otherwise. Your heart may not be mine – yet – but it is at least free."

"No." Eugenia shook her head. "It is not free, my Lord, for it is all yours. I believe it has been yours all along, but I was too foolish to understand the signs."

The Marquis held her at arm's length. "The signs?"

"My jealousy, for one thing – when you seemed to favour Lady Walling."

The Marquis began to laugh. "But I never favoured Lady Walling. It was just that she knew my father and uncle. She is a tiresome woman to whom I feel I owe a certain level of courtesy."

"But – but Bridget said that you and she were – lovers."

"Oh, my sweet foolish girl!" The Marquis exclaimed. "Have you not guessed that she lied in order to more successfully press Gregor Brodosky's suit?"

Of course. Eugenia could not believe she had been so blind. With a cry she fell again into the Marquis's open arms. Now for the first time she was truly his. For the first time she felt the passion that once she had only imagined pulse through her blood.

Her whole body shuddered at his touch. Her very soul seemed to throb with a delicious fever. Here, here in the arms of her husband was the all the romance she had ever craved.

"So you have loved me all the while?" the Marquis murmured.

"Yes, my Lord. I have always loved you."

"And I have loved you with all my heart and will love you for all eternity."

With a groan, he swept her up from the floor.

"We have a great deal of lost time to make up, my angel. What a good thing it is that I am mad with desire for you. I am going to spend this night making love to you again – and again – and again!"

Eugenia swooned as her husband carried her to the sofa.

What better place in the world was there for her to yield herself up to joy, what better place to be truly made a woman and a wife, what better place to be loved and give love in return and be certain of endless happiness than here at her beloved '*Paragon*'!